A Position
of Privilege

BY

Bernard McNeill

A Position of Privilege

First published in 2011 by B.A. McNeill for distribution through Amazon.com

ISBN-13: 978-1463654474 (CreateSpace-Assigned)

ISBN-10: 1463654472

BISAC: Fiction / Mystery & Detective / Traditional British

Copyright © B.A. McNeill 2011

All the characters in this book are fictitious, and any resemblance to actual persons, living or dead, is purely coincidental.

Bernard Anthony McNeill asserts the moral right to be identified as the author of this work. All rights reserved.

No part of this publication may be reproduced, stored in or introduced into a retrieval system, or transmitted in any form or by any means (electronic, mechanical, by photocopying, recording or otherwise) without the prior written permission of the publisher.

**MYS
Pbk**

<u>DEDICATION</u>

This book is dedicated to my wife Jill, for putting up with both me and my eccentricities for the last 38 years.

ACKNOWLEDGEMENTS

I would like to like to thank my wife Jill and my uncle, Alec Ganley for reading and correcting the text and for their many helpful suggestions.

Friday 1st December.

1.

Kevin Feeney crossed the small courtyard hurriedly. It was in the dark days before Christmas when it never really got light at all. There had been a slight snowfall late the previous evening and a hard frost overnight. His eyes were half closed against the icy needles blown by the early morning breeze and the glistening carpet crunched beneath his boots. He shivered as the bitter cold bit through his old grey overall. Two rats, foraging by the bins, paused momentarily in their hunt as the light of his torch swept over them. They sniffed the air inquisitively, decided that he was no threat to them and returned to their business. They would have to go; he made a mental note to check his bait boxes and move them to new locations. He rounded the corner of the Technology Block and undid the padlock on the boiler house door with fumbling fingers. The metal was painfully cold and he was glad to be able to release the lock and leave it hanging on the hasp. He pulled open the heavy wooden door and hopped inside into blissful warmth. His fingers found the light switch high on his left and he pulled the door shut. Yellow flame flickered behind the thick glass door of the furnace making the shadows of pipes and tools dance eerily across the walls. The boiler was oil fed and on an automatic timer. The days of shovelling coke were long passed, thank God. He couldn't cope with that now at 53, though he would never admit it when telling younger men how it used to be. He trotted down the steps and over to the pressure gauge. Spots of ice, picked up on the short journey from his house, turned opalescent and melted in his short, grey, stubbly beard.

The furnace had burned low all night, to conserve fuel, putting out just enough heat to prevent the water pipes from freezing. Sensors, inside and outside the building, constantly monitored the temperature and sent their data to a box of electronic wizardry on his back wall, which increased or decreased the activity of the furnace to keep a steady balance between them. The clock on the wall showed six twenty-eight. He stood quite still now, watching the gauge. It wasn't really his business to know how it worked, just to see that it did, but he took a justifiable pride in his responsibilities and pried into any area that connected with them. He had discussed mechanical thermal couplings and integrated circuits with the Physics teacher and enjoyed displaying his pretended thorough grasp of the essentials of control technology to third parties whenever the opportunity arose. The clock showed six twenty-nine. Not that he would ever interfere with the black box, of course, he had a manual override switch if necessary, but, as Building Services Supervisor, his was a management role. He would telephone for the engineers in case of failure. Even though he was expecting it, he flinched physically as the slow gentle hissing of the boiler broke into a roaring inferno of sound, shattering the early morning peace.

Six thirty, the control had cut in on the second. The needle on the pressure gauge climbed steadily from white to yellow and then to green, finally holding steady at 150 kPa. Six thirty-two, the pump cut in to add to the cacophony, pushing 600 gallons of hot water round the system and bringing his building to life again. He crossed the floor of the boiler house avoiding a large puddle as he went. Puddles were a problem. The floor of the boiler house was the lowest point of the building and the produce of any substantial leak usually ended up here. He climbed the steps at the far end to reach a small green painted door, just visible in the deep shadow cast by the bulk of furnace and boiler. He selected a key from his ring as much by feel as by vision, pushed it into the lock and turned it in a single movement, learned by long practice. Just a flick of the handle and he stepped into his office. He liked the sound of the word, office. It had a ring to it, and it always irked him to hear anyone refer to it as the caretaker's room. He turned on the light and blinked for it was much brighter in here than downstairs. The roar of the furnace subsided as he closed the door.

He moved quickly now, his motions automatic by the force of habit. He switched on the large electric kettle at the wall socket. It had already been filled and plugged into the socket the night before, ready for the day to start. Six mugs stood on a small table nearby, together with teapot and sugar bowl. He turned to his desk. The cleaners' time sheets were there, laid out ready, as he had left them. He unlocked and opened the key safe, took out his large bunch of keys and placed his small ring on the empty hook. He drew the bolts on the internal door, top and bottom, and moved out onto the main corridor. Striding away rapidly, he hit each light switch as he passed, pushing the darkness away in front of him. He flung open the fire doors before him and was passing through the third pair before the first had swung closed against their dampers. He reached the staff room door, unlocked it and entered.

Five fluorescent tubes illuminated immediately when he pressed the switch but the sixth flickered and failed; a little job for later. Glancing upward at the wall-clock, he knew what he would find before he saw it. The clock showed six thirty-eight. "Three minutes slow as usual", he thought, without bothering to look at his own watch to check. He picked up a straight-backed chair as he did every morning and placed it under the clock so that he could stand on it to make the necessary adjustment. Crossing to the sink, he removed the washing-up bowl, took the lid off the urn, which stood on the work-surface next to the drainer and emptied its contents away. The teachers never emptied the urn. They just kept topping it up. If he left it to them, some of the water in the urn would be three weeks old and they'd be complaining about the taste. He half filled it with a saucepan switched the thermostat to maximum and threw the socket switch.

Out on the main corridor again, he strode past the entrance to the Admin Corridor which housed the Head's, Deputies' and Secretaries' offices, to the main entrance, arriving just in time to see the headlights of the first car pulling into the car park. Mrs. Leach, undoubtedly, she was always the first. He drew the bolts, turned the lock and pulled open the door to greet her as she reached the top of the steps. "Morning, Doris." "Morning, Mr. Feeney, another cold one. My hubby had to have a good scrape of the windows before we could get going this morning, and they still froze up again. We had to stop twice." The cleaners always called him Mr. Feeney. The teachers always called him Kevin. It was the order of things. She stooped and picked a bottle of milk from the crate left on the step earlier. "Kettle's on," he called after her retreating figure as she scuttled off to brew.

He waited for the others to arrive, greeting each in turn. It was a courtesy, he said. A friendly face and a cheerful smile gave the day a better start, he said. It was his way. When they were all in, he picked up the milk crate, marched back to the staff room and placed it underneath the work-surface in the kitchenette. The urn was steaming now so he turned it down to number 2. That would keep it nicely ready for the early birds. Then he headed off to unlock the rest of the classrooms, the external doors and the perimeter metal gates before returning to his office to join his staff in the first mug of tea of the day.

His ladies knew their morning and evening duties and needed no direction unless there was something special to do. The classrooms had all been cleaned the previous evening, after the hordes had left, and the bins had been emptied. The buffing of corridors and stairs was Friday morning's work and each lady had her assigned machine and station. When they had gone, he washed the mugs and set them ready. He emptied the teapot and refilled the kettle. His ladies would want another cuppa before they left. He checked that they had all signed in on the worksheets and headed back towards the staff room.

As he stepped along the corridor he could hear the steady thumping of the photocopier turning out the day's first batch of worksheets. The beating that machine took from 42 teachers was incredible. It was amazing that it worked at all. It fell silent just as he reached the door and there were the warning three beeps that indicated a fault. When he opened the door a still figure was hunched over the machine with the side panel open staring into the works hopefully. Madeline Fraser, chemistry teacher, was a lady of his own age. She was an old fashioned teacher and totally dedicated to the kids. It said a great deal about her efforts on their behalf in that some of the girls called her Mum, though never to her face, so she was unaware of the compliment. She turned and beamed when she recognised him.

"Oh, Kevin, this dratted machine never works properly for me. I've only one more set to do. Can you sort it?"

"Give it a kick, Madeline," said a voice from the kitchenette. A tall, thin man emerged from behind the corner with a steaming mug and relaxed back to rest his rear on the radiator. "That's what I always do." said John Gerard, Head of Technology. He looked harassed despite a large smile, for he had recently joined the ranks of fatherhood and was still enjoying the pleasures of four-hour feeds.

"Good morning, Madeline," said Kevin retrieving a jammed A4 sheet from underneath the roller and closing the panel. Good morning, John," he said, hitting the reset button. He placed the last original into the feed and pressed the start button. The copier clicked and whirled into action. "Now we know, not all the vandals are kids. Some of 'em are on the staff," joked Kevin. "Most of 'em, in my opinion," said John, "If it wasn't for the kids the place would be a shambles." Madeline laughed and moved to the urn to pour coffee for her and tea for Kevin. There was a genuine camaraderie between them. John and Madeline were morning people. They liked to be up and doing and usually got in an hour's marking or preparation before briefing. They met in the staff room around seven-thirty each morning to exchange pleasantries and share a brew before going off to their respective rooms. There was usually a fourth member of the early bird group.

"Mike's late, today," said Madeline.

"Thank God for small mercies," said Gerard.

Madeline looked at him quizzically, "You two not getting on then?"

"Not so as you'd notice," said Gerard, "but I don't want to talk about it."

His face was hard now and the others thought it better not to ask further. To himself Gerard thought that few people did get on with Moran. Madeline Fraser and some of the older staff seemed to have good relationships with him, and he was always charming to the female members of staff in general; but he expected compliance with his ideas and it was not a good idea to cross him. He had a sharp tongue and a vindictive nature. He was a power in the school, a big fish in a small pond and he enjoyed it. As bursar he controlled the purse strings which gave him a handle on everybody's working life. Outside the institution he was nothing in particular, but here he was king of the hill.

"Looks like a fine morning, despite the cold," said Kevin changing the subject. "The kids should be able to go out at break time."

They spent a further 10 minutes or so in small talk, and then John and Madeline went off to their respective rooms to get ready for the day's work. Kevin marched round to the kitchens to greet the cooks arriving by the back door. He always lit the pilots on the gas ranges for them at this time. It wasn't part of his work or even necessary. They were perfectly capable of doing it for themselves. It was just a courtesy. It was his way. A large van arrived while he was there and he chatted to the driver as he helped him unload. When he had passed the time of day to his satisfaction it was back to his office to check on his ladies. They were there, finishing their tea, and he passed the work rosters over to them so that they could sign out. He liked to accompany them chatting to the door, and always saw them off with a cheery, "Mind how you go."

2.

The staff room was always crowded at briefing. St. Norbert's had been built to serve an estimated 330 pupils but now had over 600 on roll. The teaching complement was 20 when the school had opened 30 years ago, but it had now swollen to more than twice that number. Some sat in the tatty old-fashioned arm chairs; others stood or leaned against walls, while others squatted on the rickety coffee tables. Whatever resources the school possessed had not been spent on the comfort of the teaching staff. The buzz of small talk and pleasantries subsided as Mr. Price, the headmaster, entered at 8.40 precisely, and crossed to his usual position in the middle of the room under the clock, to address his staff.

"Good morning! It's lower school assembly this morning. Please get your classes down to the hall promptly. Eileen?" He looked across to his 2nd deputy who was pinning the day's cover sheet on to the board by the door.

"Margaret Hailey and Joe Stanner are on courses today. Hilary Manton is ill and is not expected back until Wednesday next. Paul Jarvis is delayed for personal reasons but expects to be in by 10 o'clock. I would like to welcome Steve and Joan who have come in to cover classes for us," she nodded to the two strangers hovering in the kitchenette, "but some internal cover will be needed as well and also some help with registers. Please stay behind after briefing if you don't have a form group."

"Thank you, Eileen." said Mr. Price, "Derek?"

The first deputy, Derek Turner was sitting on his left. "I put out Stuart Aitchison yesterday after an incident of violence, and he will stay out until his parents come to see us. John Rigby and Michael O'Donaghue were excluded on Monday after a nasty fight, but I saw their parents yesterday and they will both be re-admitted today. Can I please remind staff to get to their duty points on time? Several people were late at break yesterday, which does make life difficult if there is an incident. Can I remind all heads of department that Mock exams start next week and I need a copy of each exam handed in to me by the end of today?"

"Mike?" There was no response. Several heads turned and looked around the room. Mike Moran, the school bursar, was known for never being late or absent. For him not to be there was an event sufficiently unusual to cause to cause a buzz of comment. "Has anybody seen Mike?" asked the head. Eileen Lamb looked perplexed and said, "He hasn't rung in. If he's not here I shall have to use cover 2." There were sighs as those designated for 2nd emergency cover suddenly realised they had just lost their non-contact time. "Perhaps he's just delayed in traffic and will be here shortly," said Mr. Price. "Anyway I know he wanted to make an announcement this morning. The Local Education Authority has notified us that there is to be a full audit of all school accounts in 2 weeks time. This is nothing to worry about. We get this every three or four years. So heads' of departments need to get their stock books up to date and anyone who deals with money, budget holders, trip organisers, tuck shop manager, etc. will need to see that all their records are correct. Mike has probably spoken to some of you already, but he wants to hold a meeting next week to clarify matters. Anything else? He paused and allowed his eyes to wander around the assembled staff.   No? Right have a good day!" He waited a while in case anyone wanted a word, exchanged a few words with passing staff members and then left.

The staff took registers and class logbooks from the trolley by the photocopier and dispersed to their rooms to meet their charges. Miss. Lamb hovered nearby to make sure that all the registers were gone and that there wasn't another unknown absentee. When she was sure all the groups were covered she hurried to catch up with the rest of the senior management team

"Unusual for Mike not to be here" said Mr. Price.

He was now sitting, with his deputies, in his office. The three usually met for a couple of minutes during registration in case there was a problem which was not suitable for general publication.

In contrast with the staff room, the Head's office was opulent. A large, light oak desk of modern design took up most of one side of the room together with an imposing high back swivel chair. On the desk stood his computer and printer and a telephone console. There were 4 cream and beige filing cabinets on the left and three coffee tables in the middle. These matched the desk in colour and style. The other two sides were lined with comfortable armchairs in a clean, oatmeal upholstery, for small group meetings. In the corner stood a small curved table, with a tray and white cloth, on top of which was a coffee percolator, five china cups, a milk jug and a small sugar bowl, all matching. The room was tastefully decorated and curtained to give an air of authority and efficiency.

"And he would have rung if he could" said Eileen, looking worried. "Maybe he's had a car accident?"

"Well, if he did, it probably isn't serious," said the head, "The speed of traffic in the rush hour round here is so slow that you usually only get minor bumps and scrapes. He would still have rung in on his mobile. He's more likely to have been taken ill. I think I'll wait until after assembly and if he isn't here by then, I'll ring him at home. He lives alone doesn't he?"

Eileen Lamb nodded. "So he might need some assistance."

Derek Turner helped himself to black coffee from the head's percolator, "He seems to have been under pressure and out of sorts recently" he said. "He was having a fearful row with John Gerard on Tuesday evening on the English Corridor. I don't know what it was about. They stopped and both walked away when they saw me coming. It's unlike Gerard to lose his rag. Mike was also very rude and short with Chris Summers on Wednesday afternoon in the staff room. She was nearly reduced to tears. They were talking quietly and he suddenly said very loudly "Anyone with half brain wouldn't have such problems." A number of staff heard it. Then he walked out of one door and she ran out of the other. I thought I might catch up with him today and have a word."

"You should have said something before now, Derek, if those things happened at the beginning of the week." Mr. Price looked at him, with annoyance showing in his face. "Staff disputes only get worse if left to fester." His deputy blushed slightly. "You're on assembly aren't you?"

"Err, yes," said Turner.

"Better get going then. I'll enquire about those incidents myself." Turner left his unfinished coffee on the table. As the door closed, Mr. Price turned to his second deputy. There was irritation in his voice. "The problem with Derek is that he's a goose when it comes to confrontations with other staff. If there was a shouting match on a corridor between two seniors, it shouldn't have been left."

Eileen looked uncomfortable. "Mike has been on edge all week though," she said. "Out of sorts, is right, ill tempered even. He's hardly said two words to me all week, and he's normally quite chatty."

Mr. Price tapped his teeth with his pencil thoughtfully. "I hope he's not worried about this audit. He said he didn't have any problems when we discussed it on Monday."

"But he wouldn't, would he? He's a very proud man. If there was a problem he would want to sort it himself."

"Perhaps." said the head, "but he's also a professional man and a senior. There shouldn't be any secrets at this level and problems should be discussed if only to keep everybody informed and up to speed. He's been through audits before and there haven't been any problems. He might be ill or he may be having personal problems. Let's leave it there for now. Anything else?"

"No, I don't think so. We are a bit tight on cover, today, but we can cope" She stood and smoothed down her skirt. "I'll go and stand on the science corridor to see them back from assembly. The ninth year have been very boisterous this week."

Mr. Price sat for several minutes after she had left. Moran had been a thorn in his side since he became head 3 years ago. The bursar pre-dated his own appointment as head by many years and they saw things very differently. By the time Price arrived he was well ensconced in his territory. Price found him difficult and resistant to change but he commanded a respect among the juniors which made it difficult for Price to mould them to his ways. Price hoped he would move on, perhaps to a bursar's job in a bigger school. He even pointed out a couple of adverts for such to him. Price had made up his mind long ago that when Moran did go, he would appoint someone from outside, with a finance background. A book-keeper or secretary perhaps, someone who would work for him and report to him alone. Moran would be the last teacher bursar. He thought it would be better all-round if Moran would just go. Moran didn't go, he stayed.

His line of thought was broken by the beep of the internal phone. "Yes, Margaret?"

"I have City Finance on line two for you Mr. Price, a Miss. Bailey with the Internal Audit Department"

"Thank you, Margaret, I'll take it" He pressed button 2 on the console.

"Good Morning"

"Mr. Price?"

"Speaking"

"This is a bit delicate; we are having some problems with the preliminary figures we took off your system yesterday."

"Shouldn't you be speaking to my bursar about that?"

"Well, normally yes but this is a little unusual and I don't want to talk over the phone. I wonder could I come and see you about it, later this morning?"

"Is it that urgent, we are a little pressed today, with staff absences?"

"Well, yes, it is really. I think we should talk as soon as is possible."

"Well I should be free about 10.30 for about half an hour. Will that do?

"Yes, that should be fine. I'll see you then."

No sooner had he put the phone down, than it rang again. "Yes, Margaret?"

"I have Miss. Summers in the outer office. She would like to see you before she goes to class?"

"Very well."

It looked like one problem would not have to be sought for, it was coming to him. Christine Summers was a short and painfully thin, 30 year old, who cared for an invalid and failing mother. She was careworn, and always slightly depressed. He always felt depressed when he met her. She was always, neat and particular in her appearance. Today she wore a three-quarter length, cornflower blue dress with matching belt, and black high heel shoes. The whole accentuated her thinness and made her look anorexic. The bright colour did not counteract her doleful expression, and her blue tinted spectacles made her look positively ill.

"Take a seat, Christine." He ushered her over to the armchairs. "Coffee?"

"No, thank you." She dabbed at her nose with a small floral handkerchief, and he suddenly realised that her eyes were red and puffy. She had been crying. She sat not knowing what to say. She couldn't voice her obvious pain.

"Is it your mother?" he said softly. The emotion burst and she sobbed quietly into her hands with her shoulders shaking. He was embarrassed and felt completely helpless. His skills of management, his intelligence, and his organising abilities were of no account now. He could only sit and be there. She broke through eventually with, "She is getting worse, but that was expected. It is only a matter of time. Sometimes she hardly knows me, but sometimes she's fine."

"Can't you get more help?" said Price. "There must be ways of easing your workload at home."

"I have help to get her up and washed in the morning, and to put her to bed at night. She's becoming less mobile and she spends much of her day in her chair, so when she does try to move she has accidents. She paused, gasping for air between short, sharp sobs.

We have "meals on wheels" at dinner time, and the neighbours drop in when they can. It's the hospital visits that are the biggest problem. It takes most of the day and she has to be accompanied. I have been having a lot of time off recently."

"Yes, but we understand the reason. We're not going to pressure you on that."

"But I can't afford it." She sobbed. Every time I have a day off Mr. Moran stops my pay. I have to pay for the carers who come in each day. I am behind with the mortgage and overdrawn at the bank. Mother has no money. She never worked. She was just a housewife. I've used respite care a couple of times, to give me a rest and to help me catch up with my work, and that costs the earth. I can't keep up with my marking load. I don't think -
-"

"Mike's been stopping your pay!" Price interrupted the flow of words incredulously.

He couldn't believe what he had just heard. Obviously it would be the letter of the law. Certainly, it would be, for people pursuing their own interests. Unpaid leave was not unusual; a couple of days to finish off a special holiday or to go to a wedding, if it were abroad maybe. But for hospital visits for a dying mother! For a member of staff who hadn't missed a day in years! Such things were usually quietly glossed over. This was appalling! What was the man thinking of?

"I understand there was a problem between you two in the staff room on Wednesday, was it about this?"

"Yes." She spoke quietly now, "I didn't realise you knew about that." She was very still, and staring at him. "Has Mr. Moran, spoken to you?"

"No, I heard about it from someone else this morning. I heard he was rude?"

She sobbed again and he waited while she gathered her strength.

"He said I was having too many days off. He said I should put Mom into a home and get on with my life." The emotion took over again and she sobbed uncontrollably."

Price was angry now. He felt hot rage rising inside him at the cold cruelty of it, but he spoke gently, "That is nonsense, you know. He can't do that. I do assure you. You needn't worry about any more pay being stopped for essential hospital visits. Tell me when you have to have one. I will sort this out. Believe me. I am well aware of your service record and we will make allowances in these circumstances. He had absolutely no right to make a comment like that about your mother. I can't think what's got into him. That was a terrible thing to say.

She sat up startled and he could see fear in her eyes. "I don't want any trouble. I just didn't know what to do."

"Shh, Shh." he said, "There won't be any trouble. You're a valued member of staff and I'll see that he knows it. Now can you cope today? You are obviously very upset. Do you think it might be as well for you to go home for the rest of the day?"

"No, I want to stop. I want to take my lessons." She got up and walked towards the door. "I'm not taking liberties. The kids help. They cheer me up. You can't dwell on problems in a classroom. The kids take you over completely." She was smiling now and looked relieved. A weight had lifted from her."

He was pleased with his efforts and relieved that she was able to work; another absentee would push them to breaking point today. As the door closed he moved quickly to his desk, picked up the phone and pressed 21 on the pad. "Margaret! Christine has just left. Go after her would you. She's very upset. She'll need to wash her face before she goes to class and it might help if you could have a little chat in the Ladies. And Margaret! Let me know the moment Mike Moran gets in."

3.

John Gerard backed out of the Tech. block door laden to the point where he could barely see over the top of the pile of old worksheets and exercise books in his arms. He moved slowly over to the big continental bins by the kitchen wall. He deliberately picked the 5th bin in the line of 6, knowing that Kevin would empty his litter collection into one further down the line. Kevin was so predictable. Across the playground he could hear Kevin with his 2 stroke litter picking machine starting his first run of the morning. He planned to dump the lot without Kevin seeing him, or there would be moans about the bins being filled up the day after they had been emptied. This was his 3rd trip and he hadn't been spotted yet. Thursday was bin day, and if lots of teachers had clean outs on Fridays it didn't leave enough room for the cleaners and their rubbish for the next 4 days.

Gerard was pre-occupied; worried in fact; and when he had problems he tidied and re-organised his cupboards. It was a sort of renewal. It helped him to think and to focus his mind on his problems. His problems were no respecters of dustbin days.

"If you have to have a clean out, bring it down on Wednesday night and stack it by the bins ready to go Thursday morning." Kevin would say. "Then you don't cause problems for other people." If all the bins were full they usually caught fire. The caretaker was always handy to put them out with a hose. It was Kevin's way of making a bit of space. If the dustbin men complained, he blamed the kids.

Kevin had his ear protectors on against the noise of the motor and was concentrating. He made neat passes across the area, sucking up crisp packets and cans into the huge vacuum bag hanging off the back of his machine. He took pride in a nice clean playground and liked it clear before break time. That way you stood a chance of them using the bins around the playground. It also made it easier for the duty teachers to pick up and challenge any overt litter droppers, if they could be bothered.

Gerard watched him idly, hidden from Feeny's sight by the big bins. As Kevin approached each of the playground litterbins, he stopped lifted out the bag and tied the top with one of the short pieces of string he had cut for the purpose. Then he popped in a new one. It was usually a one-handed operation. Cellophane and aluminium didn't weigh very much, and in any case there was generally more on the ground than inside. Suddenly he appeared to meet resistance. The bag he was trying to lift seemed heavier. Gerard noticed that Feeney had to use two hands to pull it out of its casing. He tied up the top and lent it against the bin, but it toppled over straightaway on to its side. Gerard took advantage of Kevin's concentration on the bag to slip back inside the building.

Kevin went on to finish and then fetched his little pull trolley to collect the bags. He trundled the bags over to the six big bins and dropped them into the second one. He rolled the trolley back into his shed and he went off to his house to have his breakfast, without giving the heavy bag any further thought.

Gerard saw him go from the window of the Technology Block, and breathed a sigh of relief. It would be a couple of days before he noticed the half full bin and by then there would be other stuff on top of his. He returned his attention to the 8th Years who were practicing isometric drawings of the 3-d blocks that he had given them. They liked drawing and were quietly absorbed in their task. It gave him time to think, and he very much needed time to think. He was in a complete and utter mess, and he didn't know how he was going to get out it. So! There was to be an audit! That explained a thing or two. He wondered why Moran hadn't mentioned it. He had led a Ski trip to Northern Italy during the half-term break and it had all gone belly-up. He had overspent the budget and Moran was on his case. The final invoice from the Adventure Holiday Company had come and there was nothing left in the account with which to pay it. Moran wanted to know how he was going to find the money. Where was he going to find £700? The school had to pay it surely? It was an institutional debt. They might not be very happy about it, but they had to pay. Moran said he wouldn't pay. He couldn't allow people to run up debts in the school's name without agreement or budget planning. According Moran, Gerard organised the trip, collected the money, made the bookings and sorted all the details. It was Gerard's responsibility to sort out the shortfall. The invoice was in Gerard's name. Moran said, "It's you they will name in a court action, if it goes that far." That's all he needed. He and Josie had just saved up enough for a deposit. They were going to look for a house and apply for a mortgage. He stood no chance of a mortgage if he got sued for non-payment in the County Court. The trip had gone very well. Perhaps he could run another trip at Easter and make a profit? He had suggested as much to Moran. Moran said he couldn't hold the overspend that long. It had to be sorted out now.

Mr. Price stepped into the room. "Stand" said Gerard. Some of the class had noticed the Head's entry and were already on their feet. The others reluctantly interrupted what they were doing and stood up. "Thank you," said Price, waving them down. "Please continue. Good morning, John, they seem to be well on task."

"They always enjoy TD," said Gerard, "It means they don't have to think." The touch of anger was obvious in his voice.

Gerard hated people coming into his room during lessons. There was a low murmur across the room since the interruption, and he knew it would break into multiple conversations once Price left. He had lost the moment with this class and wouldn't get it back today. The management seemed to think they could just walk in and out whenever they pleased regardless of the effect on the kids.

Price was sensitive of his attitude and decided to postpone his enquiry, lest the tension between them became evident to the children. "I'm sorry to interrupt, but I do need to see you quite urgently. Could you take coffee with me in my room at 11.15 and we can sort it out then?

Gerard's attitude mellowed visibly. Obviously the head knew of his problems and was taking a hand, and he sounded as though he had a solution. He didn't sound like he was jumping on Moran's bandwagon. He wondered how Price had got hold of the information. He didn't think Moran would have told him. It wasn't his style. Moran had been here longer than most people and generally behaved as though he owned the place, even to the head. He was surprised to find that he was flattered by the tone of the invitation. Price didn't say "I want to see you in my office" he said "Would you take coffee with me in my room?" Very public-schoolish, but he was still pleased.

"Yes, Ok. There's a couple of things I need to get off my chest too. Break will be fine."

Price left and the volume moved up two levels. "Alright, settle down. Let's get back to it. I want two completed drawings from each of you by the end of the period; three if you can manage it."

Did Price know about the Ski trip? Perhaps it was something else. Perhaps he was on the carpet after all. The feelings of anger and frustration returned. OK he'd messed up, but Moran could easily cover him from another account for a while if he wanted to. Well, the man was going to have to! He couldn't afford to pay it and it wasn't right that he should be asked to pay it. It was a school trip for goodness sake, not a personal holiday. He'd told Moran as much on Monday, and a few other home truths as well. Moran said it wasn't educational, just a jolly for the sporty types. A lot more had been said and neither would be comfortable with the other for months now.

4.

10.15 a. m. and the lesson change bell rang. The quiet corridors turned into sudden pandemonium as classrooms emptied and pupils moved on to their next subject. It used to be that the teachers moved, but in modern times they liked to stay close to their equipment and resources. So 630 pupils piled out of rooms and into rooms in what appeared to be total chaos. To the uninitiated it was intimidating. An unwary visitor caught on the corridor would press up against a wall to seek shelter from the seething mass of bodies. The kids were moving rapidly in two different directions at the same time. Teachers stood at their doors supervising with piercing eye and loud calls. "Keep to the left"; "Don't run, Walk"; "Take that hat off Duane"; "Don't push". The noise subsided as quickly as it began. By 10.20 the corridors were silent again, with everyone closed up in their learning areas. Mr. Price left his normal lesson change station at the foot of the main stairs and returned to his office. He lifted the phone and dialled the number for the third time. For the third time there was no answer at Moran's house. The answer phone kicked in and he left another message. He put the phone back into its cradle and leaned back into his chair. He rested his elbows on the arms and joined his hands in front of his face. Once again the pencil tapped on his teeth in deep thought. It was an automatic mannerism of which he was totally unaware, and the cause of some merriment among the wags on the staff. For teachers simply not to turn up and throw the burden of covering their classes on to others without warning was unforgivable. People were hard enough pressed without losing time to do the work of others at short notice. He always rang people personally when this happened.

He was startled by the beep of the internal phone. "Yes, Margaret?"

"Miss. Bailey is here, Mr. Price. Shall I ask her to wait in reception?"

"No, bring her straight in please."

Margaret ushered in a slim lady in her 30's and introduced them.

"Mr. Price, Miss. Bailey."

Miss Bailey took off her blue top coat and he took it from her and hung it next to his own on the stand. She wore a short, black skirt. It was buttoned down the side with small gold buttons; but not all the way and the short split just above the knee swished and drew his attention to her trim legs. No doubt it was exactly the effect she intended. She wore a white blouse and black cardigan and of course smart black shoes. Her shoulder length hair was blond, hanging straight but with a slight curl at the end which contrasted strongly with the cardigan. Any thoughts of prettiness were quickly dispelled. Her face was square and teutonic, and her blue eyes hard and piercing. She was an authoritative figure.

"Please sit down", said Price gesturing to an armchair, "Would you like coffee, or tea perhaps?"

"No thanks, I won't, we have a problem and I'd like to get straight to it."

"Very well", said Price, "Just what is the problem? You were somewhat cryptic on the phone."

She opened her brief case and took out a brown manila folder, which she rested unopened on her lap.

"As you are aware, we notified you that we would be auditing the school accounts shortly."

He nodded without comment.

She carried on, "Well, in preparation for that one of my assistants called in on Monday and tape streamed your finance computer."

Price was unclear. These were not areas he was familiar with and he felt nervous before this obviously competent young woman. He needed to re-establish his position. He sat up straight in his chair. "I'm sorry, I wasn't aware of that. Could you explain exactly what you mean?"

"We took a copy of your hard disk for comparison with what we hold on our central computer in German Street." She could see he looked perplexed. "It is normal practice," she said "and we did arrange it with Mr. Moran."

"He never mentioned it," said Price, feeling rather foolish. "Don't you compare data weekly? I thought you had a weekly exchange of data electronically for reconciliation purposes." He understood the reconciliation process. Moran brought him the reconciliation report each week to sign, and he now felt on firmer ground.

"Oh, yes we do", she said, but things sometimes get changed afterwards and there can be errors. It's just an extra check. "It is normal practice", she said again.

"Quite" said Price, "but presumably something abnormal has come up or you wouldn't be here." He smiled to establish a more intimate contact but she did not smile back.

"Well, yes." She looked a little uncomfortable now. "There appears to a variance of about £33,000.

"£33,000", Price looked even more perplexed. "Not a large amount surely, and possibly the result of a minor error which can be corrected. After all our annual budget is over two and a half million pounds."

"Well, yes, and normally we would just look for the error at audit, but it is more the circumstance in which it was found that is of concern."

She stopped and looked hard at Price, obviously debating something in her mind.

"Go on," he said, "you're going to have to explain it to me."

"Have you ever heard the term Non-order Invoicing?" She paused again for a reaction.

"No, I can't say that I have. I sign all the invoices to pass them for payment, but the original orders are authorised by Mr. Moran. That split is an audit requirement, I understand, to prevent fraud."

"Yes. We think that it is less likely that two people will collude to make a fraudulent transaction. Normally, an order is raised for a requirement, the delivery is recorded, an invoice arrives, and is then authorised by you. You send it to us and we pay it."

Her manner was again smooth and businesslike.

"We then send a reconciliation note back to your computer electronically. That is what mostly happens, but not always. There isn't always a recorded order. Your school's electricity bill, for example, arrives after a meter reading without an order being placed. So a non-order invoice is raised and authorised. It follows a slightly different path on the computer."

She paused again and looked at him making him feel very uncomfortable then carried on:

"This system is problematic, there can be errors and it may be necessary to vary a non-order invoice after it has been passed, for example if an estimated bill has been paid in error and has to be corrected"

She paused again; the look was deep and meaningful, inviting a response. He searched for words, not knowing quite what response was required.

"This is all news to me", he said at last. "Mr. Moran likes to keep the finer details of finance to himself. My input is generally at policy and budget level. I am not familiar with the details of the system."

"But you do sign to authorise the invoices for payment, don't you?" The question was rhetorical, and she went on without waiting for an answer. "Do you read them?"

There was a long silence. His brain was racing. What on earth had Moran done to him now? He remembered those large piles of authorisations, often presented at the end of the afternoon on Friday, "Can you sign them now please. We need to catch the last post."

There was no point in flannelling. "To be honest, not always" he said "sometimes if I am very pressed, I just sign them."

They looked directly at each, neither wishing to break eye contact. It was another uncomfortable moment. The room was very still.

Price broke the silence first. "I still, don't see where all this is leading. You are going to have to be more explicit."

"This is something we are going to take up with City Treasurer. I think we have a weakness in the system. As I said there is a facility to vary a non-order invoice after it has been passed for payment. It can be varied right down to one penny. Normally this is not a problem as it is merely correcting a known error which rights itself at the next invoicing period." She was beating around the bush. She had something to say but was wary of saying it.

Price looked completely bewildered. "How does this affect my school?" he asked, "and could you put it in layman's terms." He was leaning forward, his eyes fixed upon her in concentration.

She went on, "We noticed that quite a few of your invoices were varied down to one penny after payment, and that the subsequent correction never followed, in all £33,000 worth. This means there is £33,000 missing from your accounts. We wondered if you could tell us why?

Price flopped back in his chair. There was a silence while the seriousness of her question pressed upon him, and he considered the implications. His gaze was fixed now on the floor.

He looked up again and met her continuing stare.

"I am totally unaware of any of this", said Price. "I presume you are implying there's been some form of fraud. I find that very difficult to believe."

"I am not implying anything at this stage, Mr. Price. I am merely asking the question. Is there an explanation for these transactions?

"I really don't know what is going on. If what you say is true then the only person who can explain it is Mr. Moran."

"I don't want to talk to him at this stage", she interjected sharply, "and I think we need to be very circumspect at the moment. We need you to perhaps mention to him that there is a problem and ask him to investigate it and report back. We don't want to make any accusations that might be difficult to substantiate."

"You couldn't see him now anyway" said Price. "He hasn't turned up for work this morning. We're not sure why. He hasn't phoned in either. Look! What was purchased with this missing money? That surely will indicate some explanation".

"As I said, the process used was Non-Order Invoicing, which means we don't have a purchase order to refer to and some of the invoices are unclear. However," - she opened the manila folder on her knee, - "we have telephoned some of the suppliers to obtain further information. The school bought an electric cooker, a fridge, a freezer, and a dishwasher from one supplier and £2,700 worth of kitchen units from another. There were other household payments and also some payments of which we are still not sure".

She looked up at him and paused again. Her gaze invited comment.

"They could be for the Food Technology Department" suggested Price lamely.

"Most schools lease their cookers. It's generally cheaper to maintain them that way, and you do have leasing agreements in place with your Gas and Electricity suppliers. I checked. It would be most unusual to buy that sort of equipment outright."

She snapped the folder shut. "Look! We need to do some further investigations at our end and you need to ask some questions here. I will leave this folder here for you to go through. It would be helpful if you can identify any of the goods mentioned on site. I suggest we have a meeting with Mr Moran early next week, so that we can try and clear this up before the audit proper begins."

She stood and held out the folder to him. Price had the uncomfortable feeling that she still had him in her sights as a potential target, and that she wasn't at all convinced by the suggestion that headmasters might sign payment authorisations without knowing for what they were signing. He must look to be either a crook or a fool in her eyes. He certainly felt like the latter. He helped her on with her coat and escorted her out to the front entrance. She paused at the door. "You'll ring me then to set a time and date?" It felt more like a command than a request.

"Yes, I should know more about this business by Tuesday. Let's set a time now. 10 o'clock Tuesday morning.

She turned and left without further comment.

5.

"Kevin!" Madeline Fraser waved at him from her first floor classroom window. "Kevin, can you help please?"

Kevin was walking back across the playground, paintbrush and paint in hand. He was heading for the Music Block, to paint over some unflattering graffiti that had appeared during the last few days concerning the music teacher. Whenever anywhere in the school was painted he always asked for and kept the leftovers. This gave him a good range of paint with which he could match and touch up, should it be needed. He wandered over and looked up at her.

"I'm covering Margaret Hailey, and we need the Maths test papers for Year 10 after break. Mike was supposed to photocopy them yesterday but he's not in. He must have left them locked in his office. If I meet you there at break could you let me in to have a look? Do you mind?"

"No problem, Mrs. Fraser, I'll see you there."

He moved off get on with his next planned task. He normally worked from six-thirty until 12, with a half hour off for breakfast. He also popped into the staff room at break time to take tea with the staff. It was a privilege earned by his long service. He was welcome there and he enjoyed it. At 12 he went for lunch and was off duty then until the end of the school day, when the cleaners arrived back for their evening shift. He would paint out the graffiti and then check the bait boxes for rats, and move them to new locations. The litter dropped by the children was a permanent source of food for all the local rodents and he waged constant war on them. He would then change that dodgy tube in the staffroom. That should leave him nicely placed to meet Madeline at the Finance office at the start of break.

Mr. Price was in French now covering for half an hour. He insisted that he was included on the cover roster. He thought it good for morale for the staff to see him picking up his share of cover. The group were working quietly, because he was the head. He was under no illusions though. If a junior or an outsider had been covering, the kids would, by now, be well into their favourite sporting practice, winding up the cover teacher.

He was looking through the folder of invoices left by Mrs. Bailey. It read like a wish list for refurbishing a large house: Carpets, a three piece suite, a bed; all the makings of a new kitchen and a bathroom, even tools. He could see how the individual items might slip through unnoticed among all the general invoicing over a period of time. It was only when you put the whole lot together as a package that it became obvious what was happening. The LEA had been lucky to make the connections. He wondered if they had had a tip-off. Moran would, of course, have spotted it in an instant had any of this stuff gone through the order system, but that system had been by-passed. There were a number of people who might have managed this, and he was uncomfortably clear that his own name would be at the top of any list being drawn up. There was also Moran, himself; it could be his doing. The orders were typed by Angela, a young girl who came in twice a week for that purpose. She had access to the computer, but then so did his own secretary, Margaret. Margaret ran the invoice authorisation routines and printed the authorisation slips. She passed them to Moran for checking. Moran brought them to him for signing. Then again the whole Admin system was controlled by the Systems Manager, Paul Jarvis. As Administrator he would be able to get into any part of the system. The invoices could have been kept clear of Moran and then added to the signature folder later. So it wasn't clear cut. Any combination of 5 people could have been responsible, either singly or together for zeroing the invoices after payment to hide the transactions. A lawyer was going to have fun with that. No wonder Miss. Bailey was being cautious about making accusations.

There was a noise of fidgeting and paper rustling around the room. It was approaching 11.15 on the clock and the natives were getting restless.

"O.K. put your work away, get your coats on and get ready to go out."

They needed no urging and there was a rising volume of chatter as they stretched and sorted themselves out after an hour of sitting. He moved to the door and opened it just as the bell went, and stood half in and half out of the room just as he instructed all the other teachers to do when a class was leaving a room. When they were gone he locked the door and started down the corridor to the stairs at the far end.

Kevin stood outside the Finance office and waited for Madeline Fraser to come down from class. She came round the bend in the corridor in rush. She was anxious to get what she needed and get off to the staffroom for a cup of tea before she had to go to her next lesson. 15 minutes wasn't long enough. Her progress was impeded by the last of the pupils making their way along the corridor to the door at the far end, which was one of those leading out to the playground. "Oh, good! You're there, Kevin, I thought I might have to wait for you."

"No problem, Mrs. Fraser," he said with a smile, "Your wish is my command." He selected a key from his bunch, turned it in the Yale lock, opened the door and stepped back to let her precede him into the room.

"The papers I need should be here on the - - -," her words trailed off and her hand rose to her face in shock. She staggered back and fell against the door jamb, ashen faced. "Kevin, Kevin, in there." She could contain herself no longer. She vomited down her front and her legs gave way beneath her. Kevin placed his hands under shoulders to take her weight, frightened that she would fall, and lowered her to a sitting position on the floor. He propped her up on the wall, and said "Alright, just stay there, I'll get help."

She looked up at him with horror written all over her face.

"Look in there Kevin, it's Mike"

He turned and peered into the room. The bursar was sat in his chair but bent forward across his desk with his head resting on the computer keyboard. His teeth were showing and he appeared to be smiling. There was a trail of dried blood leading, from his temple across his eye on to the keyboard and then down over the desk end onto the floor. Kevin pulled the door shut without entering the room.

He shouted to the two prefects guarding the outside door, who were staring at the scene in fascination. Thank God they couldn't see into the room from their duty point. "Come here, quick." He pointed at the one, "What's your name?"

"Asmita"

"I want you to stay with Mrs. Fraser; she's not well, OK?"

"OK"

To the other he said "Richard isn't it?" The boy nodded.

"Run to the staff room please, Richard. Say Mrs. Fraser isn't well and ask for a firstaider. Then run to Mr. Price and tell him that there has been a bad accident. Tell him that I said he needs to come right away. Got that?

"Yeah"

"Go on then, run."

He turned back to the door and removed his keys from the Yale. He selected another key and locked the lower mortise lock.

The girl was squatting on her heels and holding Madeline Fraser's hand.

"Alright, Miss?" she was saying, "Alright?"

As Price came off the stairs on to the main corridor he met Gerard coming in from the small courtyard by the dining hall. They walked the last few yards to his office together.

"I suppose you want to talk about the skiing trip," said Gerard. He had decided he had better get his side in first before Price could start in on him with anything Moran had said.

"Err" Price was taken aback and very nearly said "do I?" He recovered quickly and said "Let's get a coffee and you can tell me about it." His hand was on the door handle, when a boy sped round the corner and banged into Gerard. He knocked the teacher back against the wall and nearly fell over himself.

"What the ---,"

"Sorry, Sir, Sorry."

He was breathless with running. He steadied himself against the wall and looked straight at Price and said in between gasps,

"Kevin says can you come quickly, He says there has been a really bad accident and you need to come right away. And he asked me to fetch a firstaider for Mrs. Fraser. She's lying on the floor. Miss. Fletcher has gone down there."

"Where, Richard." Asked Gerard.

"English corridor, by Mr. Moran's office, sir."

They left him there still breathing hard and hurried through the milling pupils on the main Corridor. They met his secretary as they passed the staff room talking to a pupil. "Margaret, Come with us, please." said Price and he hurried on.

They could hear Miss. Fletcher taking charge as they approached the Finance Office.

"Madeline! Madeline! Look at me. Can you hear me! Did you fall? Where does it hurt?"

Kevin interrupted her, "She's not hurt, she's upset, she's just seen something shocking."

He turned as Price and Gerard came up. "It's Mr. Moran, Sir. He's in his office and he's had an accident."

Cecily Fletcher was on her feet, "Should I go to him?"

"No, No!" Kevin held out his hand to block her. "You can't help him. He looked her straight in the eye. She caught his meaning immediately. Best get Mrs. Fraser away from here."

Price was numbed by his words, but his authority took over. "Take her down to my office." He was suddenly aware of the child squatting at her side. "Asmita, you're to go too. Go With Miss. Fletcher and Mrs Fraser."

He looked directly at his secretary, "See she gets there. You're all to stay there. Sit in my office until I come back. Margaret, when they're there, go find Mrs. Lamb. Tell her to arrange emergency cover for

Mrs Fraser's next class. She'll have to find new classrooms for the three English sets as well. I'm closing this corridor; - and find Richard Henry, please. He was outside my office; put him in the office with the others. He is to stay there too, and nobody is to say anything to anyone. John, you stand at that end by the corner and send anyone who comes that way to the hall."

The bell went as he finished his instructions and a surge of pupils came in through the door. He raised a hand and blocked their way.

"Stop!" There's been an accident. Could you please go out again and go round by the other door. English students go and wait in the hall. Mrs. Lamb will tell you where to go for next lesson. Please, go out and go round, you can't come through here. There's been an accident. English classes go to the hall"

He beckoned to his caretaker.

"As soon as they are out, lock the door."

Kevin ushered the last few pupils out and locked it.

"You'd better show me what's happened here."

Kevin started towards the door then hesitated.

"No, I don't think that's wise, sir. It's not pretty and you can't help him. His head's all smashed in. I don't think it's an accident. Somebody's killed him. Best leave it for the police."

"You can't be serious."

"I'm afraid I am, sir. Best call the police straight away. They won't want anyone touching anything.

The door's double locked and I'll stay at the end of the corridor until they arrive."

Price considered insisting, but he saw the sense of what his caretaker had said. Instead, he turned back to Gerard.

"Do you have a class now, John?

"Yes, I've got Year 7 next." Said Gerard.

"OK you, take them and come and see me at dinnertime. We'll keep this matter to ourselves for the time being. Let's try and keep everything normal until we know what's what with the police."

The two constables arrived at 11.50. They wore white shirts with black stab vests over the top and had equipment belts with handcuffs and other things hanging from their waists. With their radios and peaked caps they looked more like the military than the police. Price saw them in his deputy's office and told them of the discovery of the body. They radioed the information back to the station and said there was "a suspicious death".

"Our sergeant is coming out, we'll need to secure the area, until he gets here." said the taller of the two, who seemed to be in charge. "and there'll probably be others coming. Can somebody show us where the body is and direct the others when they arrive."

"I'll take you down," said Price, "and my secretary will direct the others. I've sent for Mrs. Fraser's husband because she is very upset, and also the parents of the two children who were on the corridor. I think we need to get them off site in the circumstances."

"Not 'til we're sure of the circumstances," said the big policeman. "I'll need you to keep them in your office for the time being."

Kevin opened the door and they peered in at the bloody scene. One stepped over the footprints on the floor, taking care not to tread on them and felt along the jaw line below the ear. He pressed in hard to find the pulse point.

"Nothing and he's cold. Been dead a good while."

He stepped gingerly back to the door and out of the room. He put his hand on Kevin's shoulder.

"Do you know this room?" Kevin nodded.

"Just look in there, will you? Don't go in. Just stand at the door and look. See anything unusual? Anything not where it should be? Anything there that shouldn't be there? Anything you notice that might be missing?"

Kevin's gazed wandered round the bursar's office. He was regularly in here about one thing or another. The large desk was where it should be, with the computer and the telephone on top. It was an old teacher's desk from a classroom. They had smaller, more modern desks these days. There were three grey filing cabinets and a wardrobe style wooden cupboard. That was for what Moran called his "walkables" – Pens, pencils, rulers, board markers, sellotape etc. things that might go missing in a school if not locked away. There was a small grey metal safe in the corner. There was a small table with some papers in a wire tray and two dirty coffee cups, one half filled with cold coffee. Everything was as he remembered it. The tile floor was marked with dry, orangey, muddy footprints. This room wasn't cleaned last night, he thought. Moran usually left it open for the cleaner, with the snap lock up. When she had cleaned it, she dropped the catch, and Kevin turned the mortise when he came by on his rounds later. This morning he had turned off the mortise as usual when he opened up but hadn't gone in. He left all the Yale's on the offices for the occupants.

"The cleaner didn't clean in here last night," he said, "that's unusual. If she had done those footprints wouldn't be there."

His eyes wandered around the room again. There was something else, something else out of order, and something he couldn't quite see. He looked at the small table and it came to him suddenly.

"There's a statue missing from that table. It was a statue of a dog, made of metal, brass or something."

"Valuable was it?" asked the PC.

"Shouldn't think so," said Kevin, "at least not to anyone else. It was a trophy of some sort. His dog won it. He shows Labradors. At least he did, not any more eh!"

"That it then?"

"Yes, I think so. He didn't keep anything else personal here. It's just an office."

"That safe?" the PC pointed to the corner, "much in it?"

"I wouldn't know," said Kevin. "He'd keep his petty cash in there, school fund and the like. Not enough to kill for."

"You be surprised what some people would kill for." said the PC, "OK, let's lock it up till the sergeant gets here." He pulled the door to. "Lock it and give me the keys."

6.

Gareth was at home when the call came. He had taken a few days annual leave and was not due back until Monday. He had been sweeping the paths and tidying up generally for the coming winter and was very relaxed. He heard the phone ringing insistently. He knew it would be work and he knew they would want him to go in. The phone was a deep annoyance and he tried initially to ignore it, hoping they would go away. The ringing continued without abatement. Eventually he came in and lifted the handset in the kitchen. "Edwards," he said curtly. The message he received got his attention immediately, both his own children had gone to St. Norbert's school. They were both away at university now but they would soon be back for the Christmas holidays. He knew some of the staff from parents' evenings and other school events. He had also been invited to join the Governing body as a parent governor, but he had declined because of the pressure of his ordinary work. He also knew the head slightly. They attended the same church on Sundays and had occasionally chatted outside after morning service. This job was on home territory.

"I'll go straight there, then. Tell Blake to meet me there would you!"

The school was about a 15 minute drive away, in a parrot's beak of greenbelt land that stuck into the north side of the city. The aspect was therefore rural, which belied the densely constructed urban area around it. To get there, meant coping with the midday traffic through the local high street, which was only slightly better than the morning and evening rush hours. As he crawled along Gareth had good reason to be pleased with life. They had moved here some 10 years ago, transferring from London.

Inspector Gareth Edwards had started as a constable in his hometown in South Wales in the late seventies. He had always wanted to be a policeman, never anything else; but it was hardly a comfortable occupation for someone of welsh mining stock in that era of industrial strife, so he had applied for a transfer to London. He was of average height and very muscular, largely because of his love of rugby, which he now followed and when a little younger played enthusiastically. He had deep black curly hair, worn short back and sides and off the collar, as per regulation, and cut a smart figure in his uniform. He was also a very open and affable young man, with a winning smile for everyone he met and a good sense of humour. People liked him and trusted him, and opened up to him easily. This was a huge asset in his day to day work as a constable and together with his own determination to succeed led to early promotion. He also had his share of luck. Two prize herberts wearing overalls walked into the Balham Court one day, right through the court in fact, and into the Judges private chambers. Once there, they rolled up the judge's valuable Persian carpet and walked right out again, past judge, jury, attendants and policemen. The pretend workmen were long gone when the judge broke for lunch and discovered his loss. Gareth was there giving evidence in a traffic case and spoke to an ill-tempered old newsvendor outside the local tube station and just down the road from the court. The thieves had parked their van on the pavement right in front of his pitch and given him abuse when he asked them to move it. He was still seething when Gareth got to him, and turned on the charm. Normally he wouldn't have given the police the time of day, but he gave Gareth make, colour and registration details. The two brothers had used their own van and were completely gobsmacked when Gareth and his colleagues turned up on their doorstep later that afternoon to collect both them and the carpet. That little incident had not done his career any harm at all.

He had met his wife Laura, there in London, at a dance at one of the many colleges. She was a student nurse. They married and started their family in a one bedroomed flat on the third floor of a house in Streatham, near the common. Gareth worked hard. He knew that police work was 99% slog and 1% luck, and that if you didn't do the slog you didn't get the luck. He moved into CID, made sergeant and then inspector, but despite his success, they were still living in a rented two bed terraced as the kids approached secondary transfer. Life on a policeman's pay in the capital did not run to a mortgage, or very much luxury in the 1980's, in recession hit Britain. In the early '90s he transferred to Birmingham, where the cost of living and the price of property were cheaper and they could at last afford their own home. They had achieved a comfortable living and prospered. Now at 45 he felt content. The kids had done well and had given him few problems, which was astounding considering the many ups and downs and upsets his colleagues had from their kids. He spent long hours away from home at times, as did all policemen. That could affect family life badly, but Laura was a tower of strength and the centre of all their lives and held them all together. He was very proud of his family. He thought himself very lucky in that respect.

He loved living in the midland city. It was a rich and vibrant melting pot of all the races, religions and colours on earth. He remembered living in a flat in London and being surrounded by theatres and cultural activities of every sort, which on a constable's pay, he couldn't afford. He could barely afford to go to work in the beginning. Here he had music and theatre and sports and all was open to him. He was indeed content. His office was in Lloyd House in the City Centre which served as police Headquarters for the whole of the West Midlands. He was one of six inspectors on the Birmingham City Murder Investigation Unit, each had his own sergeant and they all worked under the command of Chief Inspector Mills. They worked as a unit, or formed small teams, or individually as the work dictated. When they needed other staff they drew them from central reserves or from the outlying police stations around the city. Not that murder was an everyday occurrence in Birmingham. It was no different to any other major city, but some cases went on for months and there were always cold cases to review. They never closed the books on a murder. Thus M.I.U was a busy department.

.

7.

He re-focused as he swept round the final corner and into the school car park. It was just 12.30 pm. "Bad business," he thought, "a teacher being killed, in a school, with kids on site." The police incident caravan had just arrived and was being placed, and he found a slot nearby. His sergeant was waiting for him on the steps to the main entrance

At 6ft, DS Blake was a head taller than Edwards and nodded down to him. Blake was a taciturn Yorkshire man. His conversation was always limited to the necessary and he didn't usually waste words on small talk.

"Afternoon, Sir. Good holiday?" this was positively gushing for Blake.

"Well it was until this happened, Blake. I was hoping not to see you till Monday. What have we got then?

"A Mr. Michael Moran, aged 46, school bursar and Maths teacher, found in his office at 11.15 this morning, by the caretaker and another teacher. Large head wound. It doesn't look like an accident. FME is with him now, sir. No obvious motive as yet. The office is in a side corridor, so the site is clear and contained. I have a uniform constable at the end of the corridor and another here with the van. The mortuary van has arrived and they're ready to take the body as soon as you give the O.K. Scenes of Crime are tied up but will be here later this afternoon. The people immediately involved are in the head's office with the uniformed sergeant; that's the head, the caretaker, the teacher and two children who were in the area and are aware of the circumstances. It's not leaked out to the rest of them yet but we are causing a bit of a stir and we're getting a lot of attention from the windows."

"I bet we are, Blake, not an everyday occurrence this, is it!

"No, sir."

"Right, we'll start with the scene and the FME, and then I'll talk to the head and the others. Lock the caravan up and bring the constable over with us, he can help with the statements."

Edwards didn't wait for them. He knew his way round the school from previous visits and strode off towards the bursar's office. The door was open when he got there and the FME was outside writing notes in his pad.

"Good afternoon, Doctor Stirling," said Edwards peering round the door jamb. "Hmm! Not very pleasant this then, is it? The two men had a long standing working relationship and a mutual respect for each other.

"We've had worse, inspector. At least this one is in doors and dry. Your kids came here, didn't they? Do you know him?"

"Vaguely, I think he taught Jayne, for bit in the early years. I haven't had anything to do with him recently though. Have you got anything for me?"

"He's had a heavy blow to the temple with a square-cornered object. Just the one blow. The shape of it is very clear in the skin and tissues. It would have had sharp edges. It smashed right through the skull into the brain. Must have been a very heavy blow; probably a very heavy object as well; probably metal to give such a hard, clear impression. There's nothing obvious around the body that would cause that. He would have been knocked out immediately and dead in seconds. The blood's from the scalp. It always bleeds profusely and looks bad. The real damage is inside the head. The Pathologist will tell you more. I've outlined the body on the desk and floor. You can move him when you ready."

"He'll have to wait a bit. I want photographs first and SOCO are delayed. What about time of death?

"Some time last night. I wouldn't want to guess any closer. You'll have to wait for the post mortem. It won't be a problem though. The temperature in this building is thermostatically controlled. I've had a word with the caretaker and made notes for the pathologist on the settings. He should be able to give you a pretty accurate fix. The how and the when should be straight forward enough. The why and the who will be more problematic, but that's your department Gareth." He smiled and put his note book in his pocket. Blake turned the corner, followed by two officers carrying suitcases and a photographer.

"Scene of Crime Officers, sir," said Blake, "got here faster than they thought."

"Good lads," said Edwards, "Right, I want photographs of the body, from all angles, and also close ups of those foot prints on the floor. Tape his jacket and trousers for fibres. Who ever hit him was standing over him and may have shed something. Go over the whole room for fingerprints and see what else you can find for me. Something square and heavy, in metal maybe, which might be the murder weapon?"

He turned to the uniformed officer, "Constable, when they've finished, tell the mortuary people, they can have the body and seal the room. We'll be going down to the Head's office now, but we'll take a walk back this way afterwards. Cheerio, Doctor. Happy hunting!" He turned on his heel and strode away, followed by Blake and the second constable.

8.

Mr. Price was increasingly agitated. They had been there for more than an hour and he had run out of things to say. He was not happy at the involvement of the children and had sent for their parents. They were now sitting in the visitors' room across the corridor with their parents. He had been out briefly and explained that there had been a sudden death and that their children had been nearby. He was at pains to explain that the children had seen nothing untoward and that they were not in any trouble. It was just that he wanted to keep them away from the other children for the time being and that they could take them home as soon as the police agreed. Madeline Fraser's husband was with them. He had reassured him and said she was O.K., but very upset as she had found the body. Again he said they were just waiting for the police to agree and then he could take her home. Malcolm Fraser had seen his wife briefly in the corridor outside, but the police sergeant had insisted that she return to the head's office and he to the parent's room for the time being.

"Just until she has been seen by the inspector. I'm sure it won't be long now, sir. If you'd please just wait in there."

Margaret sat next to Mrs. Fraser who was still tearful, holding her hand. Mr. Price had been out on to his corridors, and touched base with his two deputies who were also aware of the circumstances now.

"We'll need to say something to the children and the staff," he said, "They know something is going on and rumour will be rife. Send everyone to their form rooms at 2.35. I'll take lower school assembly at 2.45 and they can go off home with a letter for their parents. Then bring the upper school down at three, and I'll talk to them. Tell the staff I'll talk to them at 3.30 in the staff room. I don't know what the position is yet until I've talked to the police but I should know what to say by then"

First lunch had started on time at 12.25 and things seemed to be running smoothly. He had drafted a short letter to the parents, saying as little as possible. He regretted to inform them that Mr. Moran had died during the day and that as a mark of respect the school would be closed on Monday. The children should all return to school on Tuesday. He would clear it with the police and get Margaret to type it and copy it for distribution.

Kevin was having difficulty keeping his eyes open. It was his off duty time and he was normally in his house enjoying a nap after his dinner. Indeed he was dozing a little now in the heat and comfort of the head's office. As much of his work was out of doors or moving around the building, he found sitting in the centrally heated room oppressive. The door opened and Edwards and his team came into the room. The event was sudden and startled them all.

"Good afternoon, everyone, thank you for waiting. I won't keep you long. Mr. Feeney, would you go with my Sergeant Blake here and he'll take your statement in Mr. Turner's office. Mrs. Fraser pleased to meet you again. Sorry you've been so troubled with these circumstances." He took her hand gently and bowed a little at the waist. "Now, if you go with my constable to Mrs. Lamb's office and just tell him what happened, then your husband can take you home. I might come and have a word with you myself later, if that's alright."

He was kind and disarming and she smiled back at him. He had a way with him that gave confidence to those who were nervous and solace to the troubled. He had a natural charm of which he was aware, and used to the full in the many encounters of his work.

"Mr. Price, my Sergeant has explained about the boy and the girl. I don't think we need trouble them further. Their parents can take them home. Would you please tell them for me? And then give us minute would you, I'd just like to have a word with your secretary, before I speak to you."

When they had left he turned to Margaret and said with a smile, "Cup of coffee would be nice, Mrs. Parsons. Milk, two sugars, any chance?"

She smiled back and moved over to the head's percolator to pour. She was a well made lady in her thirties, slim and trim and smartly dressed, and Edwards was not against window shopping. He had always had an appreciative eye for the ladies but never strayed from home. He sat down and looked up at her with a smile.

"So what's with our Mr. Moran, then? Who's he been upsetting lately?"

"Just about everyone as usual", she laughed in relief. He had broken tension and she was pleased to see the burden of it go.

"He wasn't a very nice man most of the time. He was very good at his jobs, a good bursar and a good teacher, but not very nice. He used to be a lovely man but he changed in recent years. He got on very well with the older ladies. Mrs Lamb and Mrs. Fraser Liked him, but most people didn't."

She paused in her flow to hand him the coffee, "but nobody would want to kill him."

"Somebody did, though, didn't they?" said Gareth quietly.

There was a heavy silence and the oppression returned to the room. Margaret was very still.

"Please sit down." Gareth gestured to one of the easy chairs. "I understand he lived alone. Was he married or did he have a lady friend?

"He was married, but separated, not divorced. She left. He stayed in the house. She has a flat. We have her address in the files."

She was looking at her feet now. She was a lady who kept many confidences. With forty-two teachers on the staff she saw and heard a great deal but kept things close to her chest. It would not be easy for her to give up all that he wanted. The entire collection of tit bits of gossip and innuendo that might just hold the key to the search for the killer.

"Unusual that," mused Edwards, "it's usually the man who leaves and takes the flat. How did that come about?"

"There weren't any children to worry about. She told Madeline Fraser that she was bored, very, very bored. She said she wanted a more interesting life."

"Not another man then? Said Gareth softly.

"Oh, no! If you met her, you'd see that. There wasn't anyone else. She and I used to go out occasionally, cinema, coffee that sort of thing. We were friends of sorts. She was just fed up with him. He was only interested in his work and his dogs. He used to have two Labradors. He thought the world of them. He took them to shows and events, and won prizes with them. He didn't take her out much though, not at all really. She wasn't really interested in the dogs and he left her alone a lot."

"Did he have a lady friend?"

"What Mike," she was laughing again now, "I wouldn't think so. Who'd have him? He was very grumpy and no fun at all."

"What happened to the dogs? Does he still have 'em?

"No they died. First one, then the other. He never replaced them. I think that's when he became grumpy. He used to be quite cheerful at one time."

"Any trouble recently, any rows or disagreements with the other staff?"

She was cagey now, not knowing whether to say more or nothing. It was difficult for her the habit of confidentiality was well embedded.

"There have been some, but I think you ought to ask Mr. Price about it, and about the audit."

She paused but he did not interrupt the silence. He waited letting it press upon her, forcing her to continue.

"There's going to be an audit and I think there are problems, but you'll really have to ask Mr. Price about it. It's not my place to say. Mr. Moran seemed worried about it. He's been hassling staff about their accounts and upsetting some of them."

He thought it better to leave it there for now. Best not to push it too hard yet, more would come later. He stood up.

"Right, Mrs. Parsons. That'll do for now but I'll probably have another word with you later. Ask Mr. Price to step in would you."

When Price returned, he was looking more comfortable. He helped himself to coffee, but ignored the china cups and used a mug from his desk instead. He sat down on an easy chair near Gareth and shook his head.

"This is incredible; completely outside my experience, Inspector. What happens now?"

"We try to find out who killed him. Do you have anyone in mind? Anyone threatened him, any disputes with other staff that we ought to know about?"

Price shook his head.

"No, nothing like that, but he wasn't universally liked. He was opinionated and very rigid in his views. He was becoming outdated and he was not very open to change."

"So you didn't like him."

"I have only been here a short while, Inspector. This is my 3rd Year as head. I was appointed by the governors to move the school forward in very specific directions, but my ability to achieve my aims is limited by the actions of others. I have to carry people with me. Education is a very fast moving service these days. We are under constant pressure to improve and change; pressure from the Education Department, from the Local Authority, from the parents, and pressure from the media. Nothing stands still for very long and if we are not seen to be improving then we are considered to be failing. That is the world we live in. Mr. Moran was a key figure. Many of the younger heads of department found him obstructive. Every innovation has financial implications and the more dynamic and innovative staff were often frustrated by him, as was I, on many occasions. As bursar he was powerful. He had an input into spending decisions at all levels and a seat on every committee and working group that he chose to attend. He knew how to use that power to get his own way, which wasn't necessarily in the best interests of the school. People tended to curry favour with him whether they liked him or not. That wasn't healthy."

"So you're not sorry to see the back of him then?"

"Not like this!" Price looked alarmed at Gareth's blunt statement.

"I think it would have been better for everyone if he'd moved on. A fresh start somewhere else would probably have been good for him too. People in education do re-generate when they change jobs. They leave a lot of baggage behind and open their minds to new ideas. He was a problem but it is beyond belief that anyone here would have killed him."

"Incredible or not Mr. Price, the likelihood is that it was someone here who killed him. When people are murdered at work it is more often than not a colleague who is responsible. Murder is a very personal crime most of the time. Now I need to know all about him. I want to talk to someone who was here before him and has worked closely with him all the time he has been here. Who would that be? Who would you point me at?"

"That would be my deputy, Derek Turner."

Derek Turner was a tall, thin man in his early 50's. He was taller even than Blake, probably about 6ft 2 inches. He still had a good head of hair and the tinges of grey made him look quite distinguished; but Gareth noticed that he was losing it a bit at the back as he turned to close the door. Gareth expected a stronger voice, and was surprised to find that his intonation was slightly effeminate and his speech slow when they exchanged initial introductions. He sat where Price had sat and looked gangly, awkward and very nervous.

"You knew Mr. Moran when he first came to the school I understand," opened Gareth, "so you probably know him better than anyone?"

Turner held his elbow in one hand and his chin in the other. He nodded very slowly.

"Yes, I was on the interview panel that appointed him as Head of Mathematics. As curriculum deputy, I always worked closely with him."

"Excuse me, I thought he was the bursar?" interrupted Gareth.

"He started as H.O.D. Maths and for many years he was a very good one, but eventually there were problems. He became a bit jaded with teaching and he lost the enthusiasm needed to inspire others and run a department. He lacked the vision for the deputy headship but he was too young to retire and was looking for a way out. It suited the previous head to bring in fresh blood to revitalise the Maths department and gave him an excuse to move Mike sideways."

"I suppose he was bitter about that?"

"On the contrary he was delighted. He got a reduced timetable but kept his H.O.D. salary. He also got an office, a telephone, and a part-time secretary. He was given time out to train in the LEA's financial systems, and their computer systems. It was a position of privilege; to have such luxuries made him the envy of the staff."

"So that would have caused some grief, I suppose. He fails at his job but gets rewarded for it. Some people would have been very upset about that, wouldn't they?"

"Not really, I don't think many others could have done the job or would have wanted it. They would just have liked to have had the perks that went with it. You see when the Local Resource Management initiative hit schools in the late 1980's there was nobody to do it. It was a bit like when computing started to come in. The initial reaction was well it's mathematical so the maths staff can teach that, and they did. Eventually the area developed its own specialist trained teachers. Most schools couldn't see the work implications that would evolve in running their own finances. They were wooed with promises of technology, "Computer Admin Systems" and increased spending, -"you can control your own finances, make savings and spend it where you will." – That's what we were told. Some heads took on the work themselves but quickly became inundated with the rapidly increasing regulation, documentation and problems. They found themselves controlling items such as Grounds Maintenance for the first time, but then found they were only allocated two thirds of the funding that the LEA had been spending on the same task. They had to chase around to find cheaper companies to do the work, often less satisfactorily. Those that didn't crack under the strain followed their wiser colleagues and appointed a bursar, usually from within their existing staff as there was no extra funding. It became a mantra that the bursar's first job was to save the school his own salary."

"And was Moran any good at doing this. From what you've said he had basically failed as a head of Maths so why would he be any good in this new job?

"He took to it like the proverbial fish to water. He started work in September. The LEA sent documentation showing that the school had in fact closed its books the previous March with a deficit of over £16,000. They asked him to submit a plan to show how he was going to repay this amount within the next three years. He demanded copies of payments on all major areas of expenditure particularly the utilities. He found that the LEA had paid VAT on the Gas and charged the school the full amount. Despite the fact that they had reclaimed the VAT, they had never repaid it to the school. Schools are exempt from VAT he demanded an immediate refund of about £5000 and got it. Next he went after the Council Refuse Department. The school was paying them £3000 year to empty the bins. He sacked them and brought in a private firm to do the same job at half the cost. He thought of things nobody else had ever dreamed of doing. The School Meals Service put their waste in the school's bins and used the school's gas and electricity to cook the meals, so he invoiced them for it. He said they charged for the meals and had to expect to pay the costs involved in running the operation. Within 6 months he didn't owe the LEA a penny; in fact they had paid him an extra £4000. His final coup that year was to uncover the fact that the LEA finance department had in fact paid an examination board their exam fees twice a couple of years previously. He demanded a refund and got it, leaving City Finance to try and recover the cost from the exam board. At the end of the year he carried forward a balance of nearly £30,000 into the new financial year. He was flying high. When he started most people thought he was quite brilliant."

"So he re-invented himself as bursar and didn't upset anyone at all?"

"Well I don't think Kevin was too pleased with him."

"Who's Kevin?"

"Kevin Feeney, Kevin's the school caretaker. He called Kevin in and told him not to place any more orders with the City for repairs and maintenance. When Kevin protested he wouldn't tolerate any opposition on the matter. He told him, - "The City doesn't employ any workmen. When you ring the city to get them to repair a broken door, they don't send somebody out to do it. They send a subcontractor. They then add 10% to the bill as their service charge"-. He said – "We are going to go straight to the contractors ourselves. You will report all repair jobs to me and I will decide who to call" -. Kevin went to the Head, but the head backed Mike. I think he felt he had to support his new bursar. I know Kevin was very upset at the time. The two have never got on much since. Kevin felt that his territory was being invaded, that he was no longer his own master. He felt that things had changed and that he was now working for Mike Moran, which indeed he was in a sense."

"You mentioned a part time secretary?"

"Angela Shilton, Yes she works in his office on Tuesdays and Wednesdays. She's a young mother and only wants part time work. It suited us because we needed someone to type the orders and handle some of the filing for Mike."

"Mr. Price mentioned that Mr. Moran had upset some of the Heads of Department, how did that come about?"

"Well, when new young HOD's are appointed they want to make their mark. They come in with fresh ideas and unless they get Mike on their side.... Sorry I keep talking as if he's still alive. Some of them found that they were held back and couldn't progress. Mike had the knack of finding money from other budgets when it suited him or arguing that a project didn't justify the expense. In the end People felt that he was the governing factor not the worth of the project."

"So he had the power to kill their projects and they resented it."

"Not on his own, these things always go to the Heads of Department working group which I chair. He has come in for some criticism and opposition in recent years, but he always fought his corner and won his argument. As chairman I usually support the status quo whenever there are disputes. I don't go with change unless they are all agreed on it."

"So who do you think was so upset with him that they decided to kill him?"

Turner was aghast.

"That's impossible, Inspector, No one here would do that."

"Of course they did, Mr. Turner, of course they did. The man was powerful and had favourites. You said so yourself. If they were in with him he found the money. If they weren't in with him, then there wasn't any money. That's a recipe for anger isn't? For rage even? If somebody is constantly thwarted and they become enraged that's a motive for murder. Now you are going to tell me about everyone he has upset in this way in the last 6 months."

9.

Detective Sergeant Blake was an intimidating man. Many had found him so. He rarely smiled and rarely spoke, keeping only to essentials. He had short auburn hair, razor cut and steel blue eyes which stared straight through you giving the strong impression that he knew all the answers before he asked the questions and a great deal more besides. It was sufficient to unnerve many a potential liar and bring the truth tumbling out. He and Edwards were complementary and worked well together. He sat holding him self very straight in a military manner with his hands joined before him on the table, his notebook and pen to one side.

Kevin was uncomfortable and was telling himself not to be as he had nothing to hide but he knew that wasn't true. There were things he did not want this man to know, personal things to do with him and Moran. They had been through the bones of it again but Blake was still probing.

"So why wasn't the office cleaned?"

"Probably locked," said Kevin, "All the offices are double locked. The office people only have yales. I have yales and mortises. That way they can keep the rooms locked when they want to during the day. They usually leave the catch up when they go at night so the cleaners can get in to empty the bins and mop the floors. The cleaners drop the catches when they've finished. I open up the mortises in the morning and lock them last thing at night. You'll be able to ask Ivy yourself in a bit. She'll be back at a quarter to four."

Blake nodded picked up the pen and wrote a little more in his notebook.

"Those orange, muddy footprints, where do you think they came from?" he continued.

"From outside," said Kevin, "We're having some work done just outside the entrance door at the end of the corridor. There's a little wall there, which the kids kicked down. It's being rebuilt. The ground's all churned up and there's spilled sand. It was raining yesterday afternoon, so somebody must have walked through it and down the corridor to the office. Ivy cleaned that corridor last night."

"You said there was a statue missing?" Kevin had described the bronze dog trophy in detail twice already and was about to start again but Blake carried on.

"What else? What about his briefcase? He must have had papers to carry? Did you take it?"

Kevin sat back and was speechless for a second.

"I didn't take anything. I didn't touch anything. I just closed the door." Blake raised a finger to quieten him.

"You might have taken it for safekeeping. So where is his briefcase?"

"He didn't have one." Kevin was still agitated that he might be being accused of something and the words came pouring out.

"He had a holdall, a sort of sports bag. A big green holdall. He kept all his things for the office and his classes in it. Exercise books and the like. He always had it with him. He carried round with him. He was never without it."

"Not there now, is it?" said Blake. The eyes stared at him again demanding an answer. Kevin couldn't understand how he had not noticed the missing bag. It was as much part of Moran as his orangey coloured sports jacket with the leather patches on the elbows and his grey flannel trousers. It was part of his uniform.

"It's not in his classroom or the staffroom, either," offered Kevin. "I'd have noticed if I'd have seen it lying around."

"So it's missing." said Blake, "anything else you haven't mentioned that might be missing? He paused and looked directly at him again. Kevin felt his cheeks glow red. He was hot and flustered and not clear what Blake meant. Blake went on. "His keys, what about his keys?

"They must be in his pockets," Kevin wasn't thinking now, just saying what came into his head.

"We found his car keys, and his house keys," said Blake, "but no school keys."

"Perhaps they were in the bag?" suggested Kevin.

"Perhaps, they were, but we don't have the bag do we?" Blake closed his book and stood up. "We may want to talk to you again Mr. Feeney." The interview was over. Blake turned and walked out of the door without any further word.

They walked down the admin corridor in silence, Blake leading with Feeney a few paces behind. Mr.

Price came from his door and joined them. Blake went on into Price's office without a glance at either of them. Kevin and his head stood together. Both were tired and stressed with events.

"We're clearing the school early Kevin. They've said it's ok for the kids to go, but they want all the staff to stay. Can you keep the cleaners in your room when they arrive? Tell them to leave the work for tonight. Nothing's to be touched. We'll be closed on Monday but they want all the staff in as usual. It will help if you could be around as the children leave."

"Right, sir."

Price went out into his school to see that the second lunch sitting was going smoothly. He couldn't sit still now; he needed activity, and he needed to be seen. The head in his school was the authority figure. If he was there, involved and visible, others would function. They would do their jobs and the school would run.

It was just turned 1.25 p.m. when Kevin went back towards his house. He decided to give his delayed lunch a miss and wait until teatime. He was still agitated and unsettled from Blake's questioning. Blake had not accused him of anything but had left him feeling guilty and suspected. He was very upset. As he passed the bins he noticed that the lid was up on the end bin. He lowered it and checked the next one in line. The two end bins were both were half full. The teachers were clearing old papers again, and just after the bins had been empted. He would run out of space before the bin men came again next week. This was always annoying, but with today's events and his emotional turmoil after his interview he felt very angry and put upon. He speeded his pace determined get to his house and return with matches and hose pipe.

10.

Edwards and Blake were comparing notes in the police incident van in the car park. They were joined by the constable and the sergeant, who told them that the SOCO had finished. There were plenty of finger prints, mostly old and smudged; those that were useful would have to be eliminated. Blake phoned in to Steelhouse Lane and asked for them to send three finger printers back about 4. o'clock. He would need to do the whole staff for the elimination process.

"Do you want the Major Incident Room at Nechells, Boss?"

"No this one is in house. Our man is close and can't run. He has a job, commitments, maybe a wife and family here. We'll handle it ourselves and set up a base at Mere Green.

He had rung the local station at Mere Green earlier and asked for a small incident room to be allocated and also help with conducting initial interviews. He knew that the local station wouldn't be heavily staffed so he had rung the Operational Support Group for more bodies.

In the corner was seated a young and quiet man, who listened attentively to his superiors. It was Detective Constable Singh's first day in CID and he had been dropped into the proverbial deep end. He was the help from Mere Green. He had expected to be making the tea for a month but was told half way through his first shift to get down to St. Norbert's School and report to Inspector Edwards. He didn't find out why until he got there and was somewhat overawed to find himself on a murder investigation team. So far no-one had given him anything to do. So he sat and listened. Gareth was talking to the uniformed sergeant.

"We just want a brief outline of their movements from midday yesterday to when he was found, and when they last saw him alive. Do they know why anyone might want to harm him? That sort of thing. They can all go home then. We can follow up on any interesting detail over the weekend or on Monday."

"What about CCTV?" asked Singh, making his first contribution to the discussion?

"Not very hopeful," said Sergeant, "they've got nine cameras but 4 of them are dummies, including the one that points at the door where our man went in. I've got the tape though. We might have caught him going out of another door, but so did a whole lot of other people. So it's not going to be much use till we know who we're looking for."

"Right, Singh," said Gareth, "that's you. Go through that tape for the last 24 hours until you know it backwards. If we dig up anything later that relates to it I shall expect you to point it out."

He turned back to the sergeant. "And we'll need to search the whole of the building and grounds. See if we can find the statue and the bag anywhere about. We'll leave you and your boys to organise that with OSG when they get here. Blake and I are going to see the widow and have a look at his pad. O.K? And tell the mortuary team to take the body.

We'll bring his wife up for the formal identification in an hour or so. Can I leave you to phone the press office? We don't want a conference for this, just a release. Say he was found dead in suspicious circumstances and we are investigating. If anyone knows anything, get in touch. You know the sort of thing. Keep it low key."

He was looking through the window of the van as he spoke. He saw Kevin coming round the corner of the building by the service lane that lorries and vans used to get to the back by the kitchens. He watched him attach the hose to a tap on the wall and go back round the corner. He continued to watch through the window as he spoke.

"We're looking for his school keys by the way. They're missing too. It'll be a largish bunch. As bursar and site manager he has the same set as the caretaker, keys for everything. We'll need a uniformed constable on overnight. Whoever has those keys can get in anywhere, and if they know the alarm codes they'll have a free run."

The air over the gym roof shimmered like a summer heat haze, he missed its significance at first, but then a thin wisp of smoke spiralled up into the shimmering air.

"Quick, he's burning something! Stop him!"

He ran out of the van, followed by the others. They galloped for the corner of the gym, ran along the side, passed the dining room and kitchens and rounded the next corner together, to find Kevin standing with his hose pipe in front of a burning continental bin. Kevin stepped back startled by two uniformed and three plain clothes officers charging at him from around the corner.

"Put that out! Put it out now!" yelled Blake. Kevin stood rooted to the ground. He was stunned. He couldn't move. Blake grabbed the hose from him. It had a pistol grip and trigger mechanism which he squeezed immediately and directed into the bin. Clouds of white steam rose up into the air.

The officers were all breathing heavily after their exertions and stood without speaking, all looking at Kevin. He came to himself and the first thing that he could think of was the old excuse, the one he always gave the bin men.

"It's the kids. They drop a match in the bins for kicks sometimes."

"I don't think so, Mr. Feeney." said Gareth. "We saw you set the hose up. This is a crime scene and you might well be destroying evidence. Now I want you to go down to the police station with my DC Singh here and wait until we come and see you in a little while. O.K."

Kevin protested that he had already been interviewed.

"Now don't cause a fuss, Sir." said Blake. "I said we might want to talk to you again. You're not under arrest, just helping us with our enquiries."

He turned to the Constable in dismissal.

"Singh, take him to Mere Green and put him in an interview room 'til we get there. Give him a cup of tea."

Hardeep took Kevin by the arm and led him off to his car. They were conscious of a hundred pairs of eyes watching them from the upper windows. Gareth waited until they turned the corner then addressed the uniformed Sergeant.

"Sergeant Young, as soon as OSG get here I want these bins emptied and gone through with a fine tooth comb, got it? I want a list of everything in them cross referenced to which bin it was in and how far down it was."

11.

45. Regal Road was in the better part of Erdington on the Sutton Border. The house was tatty and weather worn. Peeling paint hung in little petals from the window sills, and the front garden was unkempt and weedy. It was a fairly good semi-detached, on the large side with an extension over the garage to give a fourth bedroom. It was a sorry contrast to its neighbour which was smart and well cared for in a brightly painted livery of red and white. Next door also boasted a scrolled wrought iron gate painted in jet with golden tips on the scrolls. Blake and Edwards pushed open the plain little wooden gate to Moran's house and it creaked in protest. The door was lavatorial green with triangular glass panels in a semi-circular arch in the top third, one of which was cracked.

"Not exactly house proud, our Mr. Moran, was he Blake."

"No, Sir."

"Got the keys, have you? Go on then."

There were four keys on the bunch, two mortises and two Yales. Back door, two for the front door, and the garage, guessed Gareth. Blake tried each in turn. None of them fitted.

"Well, then there's a puzzle. Blake. Where are his house keys and where is the house that these fit?"

Blake didn't answer this question, but responded, "Do we want an entry warrant? Take the door down?

"No, not today, Blake, maybe tomorrow. Let's go see the separated Mrs. Moran. Perhaps she might help us out. Eh? But first we'll have a word next door."

They retraced their steps down the dirty slabbed path which was half covered with leaves from a plane tree on the pavement outside the hedge and pulled the squeaky gate closed behind them.

The bell was answered by a short, plump old lady with a shock of white hair, wearing a red apron and primrose yellow house gloves. She opened the door nervously on a chain and peered at them. They showed her their identification and explained that her neighbour had had a bad accident at work. They need a little information about him. She admitted them grudgingly into her lounge to sit on a chintzy flowered settee in a room from another age. It took Edwards back to his childhood, back to the front room of his mother's house in Swansea, which was for special times and visitors. They were ordinarily not allowed in there. Christmas and Easter and when an auntie came to stay maybe, but otherwise it was forbidden territory. The mantel was decorated with porcelain statues, obviously prized; Wedgwood's "Silks and Ribbons" was one. He recognised it as one his mother had had on her mantle. The curtains matched the chair and settee covers and there were little lacy drapes over the arms and backs of the suite to catch any spills or hair grease. There were landscape prints on the walls, and a ticking clock which punctured the silence while they awaited her return with the inevitable tea trolley.

"Very good of you to see us Mrs. Cartin," said Gareth as she poured. "Lovely house you've got if you don't mind me saying, and your garden is very trim even for this time of year. 'Fraid mine's full of leaves, just like next door."

"I have a local gardener who comes every Wednesday," she said, "The garden is beyond me now, though I used to love doing it. I don't see how I can help about Mr. Moran." She passed the cups in a slow and measured fashion to avoid any spills in the saucers. "I don't really see much of him, these days."

"He does still, live here, then?" said Edwards. The clock chimed the quarter hour. It was a quarter past two.

"Oh! Yes, I see him from time to time. I saw him on Wednesday evening. He doesn't speak though. He keeps himself to himself since his wife left. You know she left him? I think it must have affected him very badly. But things were not right for a long time before that and you could see him change."

"Change? In what way?" Edwards took another biscuit from the tray. "Lovely biscuits, these by the way, your own baking if I'm not mistaken" He smiled at her and she softened visibly under his appreciative comments.

"When they first moved in they were a lovely couple. They were newly wed and very much in love, always chatty and friendly, especially him, and just happy. That was about 20 years ago. They wanted children and tried for a long time, but it didn't happen. He built the extension because he wanted to have a large family. He used to talk of having four, two boys and two girls. I think it soured the marriage. Gradually they grew apart. He took to his dogs. He used to keep beautiful dogs. He toured the country showing them when he wasn't at work. In the end they just lived in the same house, but didn't have much to do with one another. He changed. He lost interest in the dogs and stopped showing them. Very sad really and finally she just left. She's not far away, I see her sometimes shopping. She nods at me, but she doesn't talk. She never visits him. She wouldn't be welcome anyway."

"Why's that, then?" Gareth waited for the gem he knew would follow.

"She deceived him. More tea, Inspector?"

"Oh yes please," Gareth held out his cup to be refilled then guided her back.

"Another man then, was it?"

"Oh, No! Nothing like that. You see she didn't want children, ever. He was desperate for them. She hid it well. They both went for tests and things and the doctors said there was nothing wrong with either of them and no reason why they couldn't, and they kept trying. He was always talking about it. Anyway it all came out. She didn't want children. She went along with all the rest and just pretended because he was desperate for them. I think she had already made up her mind that she wasn't going to have one, not at any price. There were rows for a while and then they just grew apart and got on with their own lives."

"Why didn't they divorce, Mrs. Curtin?" Blake looked bemused by the story she had told them as if he couldn't quite believe it. It didn't seem logical to his ordered mind.

"Oh no! That wouldn't have been possible. He was catholic you see. 'Till death do us part' and all that. He couldn't divorce her. I once said to him that he could get an annulment if she never had any intention of having children. I'm sure that's right, I had an aunt who was a catholic, but he was horrified by the idea. Wasn't in him. He just died a bit more each day. He went from being happy and cheery to being sad and morose. And then she left."

"When was that." asked Gareth replacing his cup on the trolley.

"Oh, about 3 years ago. I saw her go, suitcases and taxi, and she was gone."

12.

"Mrs. Moran? Inspector Edwards Birmingham City Police" He held up his warrant card for her to read. "And this is Sergeant Blake. I wonder could we come in and have a word? I'm afraid Mr. Moran has had an accident."

Elspeth Moran lived in rented accommodation on the second floor of a large detached house in Erdington only three or four streets away from her former residence. Gareth had got the address from Price's secretary who had it in case of emergency. The house would have been a luxury home for a man of business 25 years ago but was now 4 self contained flats, two up, two down. The loud music from the down stairs flat suggested a student occupant, and she closed the front door against it. They followed her up the stairs to her sitting room. It was a plain but homely room and it was furnished with what had once been good quality furniture.

She sat perched on the edge of the dark old-fashioned sofa, with her hands clasped around her knees. Her face was care-lined, and she looked older than he guessed her to be. The impression of age was encouraged by the thin wire spectacles that she wore and the fact that her hair was tied in a bun at the back of her head. She looked like a little old granny, yet she couldn't have been more than about 43. She was anxious and his information about an accident obviously concerned her greatly. She still cares for him thought Gareth.

"May I?" he said pointing to a chair. She gestured him to sit. Blake sat at the small dining table in the window without waiting to be asked and took out his notebook.

"Was it a car accident?" She looked down at her feet. "I expect so; he always drives too fast. Is he badly hurt?" She looked up and switched her glanced from one to the other wondering who would answer.

"No, not a car accident," said Edwards, "But he was very badly hurt. Mrs Moran, There's no easy way to say this. I have to tell you that you husband died last evening."

Tears welled up in her eyes and she sobbed uncontrollably into her hands. They sat like that for some minutes with only her sobs breaking the silence. Edwards wished he had brought a lady PC, but he hadn't expected such a reaction from a separated wife of three years standing, especially as she was the one who left. Sadness maybe, maybe regret, but not this. She still loved him. She found her hanky from her skirt pocket and wiped some of the tears from her cheeks. They were replaced immediately and she continued to cry giving them no notice. She might have been alone. Blake and Edwards looked at each other helplessly. Finally Blake stood up, crossed to the sofa and sat down beside her. The big policeman said nothing, but put his arms around her and cuddled her. She leant towards him and let him do so. Edwards was astonished. He had never seen the Yorkshire man behave like this before. He was usually so undemonstrative, so uncommunicative, so stand-offish. This was a side of Blake that was new to him. In time her sobs subsided and she pulled away dabbing at her face with the handkerchief like a bird pecking seed.

"I'm sorry to be so silly, he was everything to me." She looked up at Edwards, startled by the thoughts racing across her mind. "Why are you here? They would send a uniformed policeman surely; in normal circumstances? What's happened?"

"We believe your husband was murdered, Mrs. Moran." Edwards was intentionally blunt and watched for her reaction. It was one of complete disbelief.

"That's impossible! No-one would want to kill Michael, he was a lovely man. Everybody liked him! You must be wrong about that."

"No. I'm afraid not," said Edwards. "Mr. Moran was violently attacked and killed in his office last night. We don't know why or by who yet. Are you his only relative?" He waited for her to nod in affirmation.

"We need to contact people you see, and to find the next of kin."

"That would be me." Elspeth was recovering her composure now. Her face still showed great distress but she had stopped crying.

"His parents are dead, and he had no brothers or sisters. There isn't anyone else to tell. I am sorry, I haven't offered you anything. Would you like tea?" She needed to be doing something.

"Blake can do that, if you like." Edwards nodded at his Sergeant and towards the kitchen, but she stopped him with a hand.

"No, I'll do it; you can come through if you want to carry on talking."

She busied herself with the cups and kettle making small talk to occupy her mind and give pause to her thoughts. The kitchen was large; probably a former bedroom and it had a big oval dining table, around which they now all sat.

"I would like you to tell me about your husband. We need to understand him if we are to find who did this. Everything and anything, you never know what might help. You're separated aren't you?

"Three years now." She paused and then added, "I left him."

Edwards went on "But you obviously still have affection for him; why did you leave?"

"He didn't love me anymore. He fell out of love." Then she was lost in her own reverie, talking aloud but not obviously to them.

"We were so in love when we were married; completely at one with each other. It was a marriage made in heaven. The first few years were everything I'd ever dreamed of since I was a girl. He was kind and attentive and made me laugh. There were always little surprises and presents. He didn't need a reason. He just wanted to please me. We had brilliant holidays. We loved walking in Wales and Scotland. We camped. We read, and talked about the books we read, and he was so funny. He had a great sense of humour. Those first few years were the best years of my life. Then he started talking about children. The whole idea terrified me. I saw my mother give birth at home – 3 times. She said it was natural and that it should be at home. She wouldn't go into hospital. People did that more in those days. The last one killed her. I couldn't have gone through that. I grew up dreading the very idea of giving birth. The thought of it made feel physically sick. He couldn't understand my feelings, and I couldn't explain them to him. Anyway I wanted him to myself. I didn't want to share him, and I had my career. I was a nurse and I wanted my career just like he wanted his. I was going to be Sister and he was going to be a Headmaster." She was smiling as she ran over the memories in her head. She was staring fixedly into her tea and was enjoying the replay of an old movie that had been played many times before. Her expression hardened, and she spoke harshly.

"but he wanted children! I wasn't enough for him. I played along, I said we were trying, but I made sure it didn't happen. He said we should go for tests. I wouldn't but he went anyway. They said he was O.K. so he wanted me to go. I was on the pill from a private clinic. We had the same doctor so I couldn't have asked him for them; and I couldn't have the tests because they would have seen through me straight away. For a long time, I wouldn't go, but he kept on and on about it. Eventually I agreed and came off the pill for a while before the test. It was a risk but I got away with it, then I went straight back on the pill. The tests were fine. There was no reason we couldn't conceive. So we kept on trying and I kept pretending, until the day he accidentally found my pills. So then he knew it wasn't because we couldn't, but because I wouldn't. There were discussions, and arguments and rows. Then he stopped loving me. He left me slowly in bits and pieces. He spent more time at work. He went to the pub more often. He worked in his study and in the garden and he left me more and more alone. He bought two wretched dogs and started showing them. He transferred his affection to them. It was like they were the children I wouldn't give him." There were tears in her eyes again and she stopped speaking. Edwards waited a little but was anxious for her to continue.

"They died didn't they?" He prompted.

"No." She sat up disdainfully. "They didn't satisfy him. They couldn't, he wanted children. He sold one and kept the other for a while then he gave it away to someone. He drew further and further away, into himself. He moved into one of the other bedrooms. He cooked his own breakfast. He had lunch at school, and went to cafés and pubs for his evening meal. I still did the laundry and the ironing. That became our only point of communication. We just occupied the same space. In the end it wasn't just the silences. It was worse than silence. Silence can be benign, comforting even. When he was in the house, there was an atmosphere. You could feel it, touch it, and cut it with a knife. He could create a black depression through the house that you could taste. Sometimes I used pray for him to go out. Finally I lived completely alone so I left."

Her face was gentler now. "But I never stopped loving him. I still do. I always will. I had hoped he might change. I hoped he might miss me and come back to me, one day. He never did."

She dropped down into her inner self again and stared once more into her empty teacup. The new silence was oppressive. Edwards had some inkling of what she must be talking about, though the pain of an uncommunicative marriage was completely outside his experience. Silently he thanked God for it and hoped it would remain so. He also knew that as a man, he could never really understand her terror at the idea of childbirth. He broke into her reverie with the cold water question. It was always the question that broke silences and atmospheres and brought everyone back to hard reality.

"Do you know if he had any enemies, anyone who might want to kill him?"

She gathered herself up visibly. She had accepted the fact of his death and was back in control. Despite the upset, she had strength, and character, and stubbornness. She would not give in to her grief and her anger was just below the surface.

"No, no, No! It was just me he treated badly. With everyone else he was happy and friendly. He would always help out or do a favour for someone if asked. He used to chat over the fence to the old lady next door. He was soft with people. All his friends that I met from his work liked him. He never complained about anybody. It was just me he was angry with. No-one would want to hurt him, and I never did. I love him. "Do you still have keys to the house?" Gareth interjected.

"No, he changed all the locks when I moved out. He let me have my things and some of the furniture, anything I wanted really, but he would never let me back in. I would leave messages on his answer machine and he would phone me and talk a little, but he would never let me back in, neither to the house or his life."

"Mrs. Moran, I have to ask this you understand, for elimination purposes. I will be asking everyone who knew him. Where were you yesterday afternoon and evening?"

"I was supposed to be with Michael. I needed to talk to him. We had arranged to meet for a meal. I had a hair appointment at three o'clock and got home about five. Then I had a bath and got ready and went to the restaurant. We arranged to meet there at seven, but he never turned up. I waited until eight and then came home. I was very angry with him. I thought he had stood me up. I never imagined --." She started to cry quietly again.

"Which hairdresser did you go to, in the afternoon?"

"Mario's, on the High Street."

"And the restaurant, where was that?"

"The Bengal Garden, in Boldmere, it was his favourite. We often used to go there, when we were together."

"Why were you meeting, Mrs. Moran? You know, just for the record. You've been separated for three years. It must have been important?"

Edwards was conscious of the time passing and he needed to return to the school before 4 o'clock. He checked his watch. It was just 3.30 pm.

"I wanted him to sell the house. The mortgage was paid by both of us and we are still married. "I've been trying to get him to sell it. I'm entitled to half and I need the money. He wouldn't sell though. I thought it was to spite me, because I wouldn't give him children. I can't work now since I hurt my back. I have a small pension but it's not enough. The money from the house would have made a big difference, but he wouldn't sell. He agreed to meet me and talk about it last night. I suppose I'll get the house now?"

"You would need to check that with a solicitor, but I would think so. Right, I think that's about it for now. Thank you for being so frank with us. It all helps to build up the picture of what may have happened. I wonder if you could do one last thing, though. This will be difficult for you. We have to have a formal identification, you see. Would you go with Sergeant Blake here down to the mortuary and do that for us? From what you've said there isn't anyone else we can ask."

Elspeth smiled and nodded. "My last service to him, isn't? It'll help with closure."

13.

It was raining again as he pulled into the school car park. The iron gate to the car park was rusty and padlocked back. It didn't look as though it was ever closed. It was a cold, icy December rain that chilled him as he walked towards the front entrance. It was already dark and lights blazed out from all over the building. There was a constable he didn't know on the door who checked his identity.

"They're doing the interviews in the main hall, sir, and the fingerprinting in the dining hall. Some of the staff have left and the rest are waiting in the staff room to be seen."

"Where's Sergeant Young?" Gareth was appreciating the warmth of the centrally heated building, but still shivering and rubbing his hands together against the cold.

"He's in the deputy's office with the OSG commander, Sir."

"Thanks, Constable." Gareth strode along the admin corridor to Turner's office and entered shedding his black overcoat. He dropped it on a chair and sat down next to it.

"Right, what's been happening here, Young?"

"Quite a lot, sir. We've got the holdall. It was in the second bin."

"The one Feeney was burning?"

"No, Sir. That was the fifth bin. Ours was at the other end of the line."

"So what was he burning?

"Nothing sir, as far as we can tell. Out of date test papers and work sheets, it seems. There was nothing of any importance in any of the bins except the second one. In the first were 6 bags from the cleaners last night. We've got them in Feeney's room by the way Sir, the cleaners, I mean, not the bags."

Gareth grimaced at the lame attempt at humour.

"In the second there were eight smaller plastic bags, just like the ones in the playground litter bins. They probably came from them this morning, because the main bins were emptied yesterday and Feeney does a playground run every morning. Bins three and four were empty. Bins five and six had loose papers in them.

The bag in question was half way down bin two. It had the green holdall and a few bits of other litter." Young paused and picked up his mug of tea to take a drink.

"So, Sergeant! Don't keep me in suspenders! What was in it?"

"Sorry, Sir. There was a statue of a Labrador dog on a metal stand and there was blood on the stand. There was a towel over it. Underneath there were some papers and files, a text book and a few exercise books. There were also two bunches of keys, one large bunch inside, probably his school keys, and a smaller set in the side pocket, probably his house keys. We've sent the lot over to the forensic lab in Highgate. We might get some prints but Johnny wiped the door handle before he left so he probably wiped the dog as well"

"Do you think the statue was the murder weapon?"

"Oh, I would say so, Sir, Yes. The dog's body is hand size. You could pick it up like an electric iron handle, and then the stand is very heavy, so it doesn't fall over I suppose. If you were to hold it like that," Young raised the imaginary statue to demonstrate, "and crack someone on the head, you would do a lot of damage."

"We've already found one set of house keys," said Gareth, "but they didn't fit the door to his house. Perhaps we'll have better luck with this set. What about the site, Commander?"

"Well we've collected and bagged and listed a lot of stuff from the playground, the classrooms and the corridors. Anything that looked in anyway out of place, but to be honest I don't think there's anything relevant. We just collected it in case. I think it's all old tat. The only thing that might be connected was a pair of trainers. They were thrown deep into the bushes by the main gate."

"Why might they be significant?" Gareth was listening intently to his officer now

"Well they were together and there were two of them. You usually only find one old shoe or sock or slipper as rubbish. Don't usually find a pair and these weren't that old, still usable, so they might have been deliberately hidden. They've gone over to Gooch Street as well. We should get some DNA off them and some fibres. That might be useful if you can find anything to match them to, and they'll check the sole patterns against those in the office and records."

"Not a lot is it? Anything else?

"We've checked some of the statements taken so far. Moran was teaching a class until 3.15 p.m. He was seen drinking tea in the staffroom at 3.40 p.m. and two people saw him go into his office at 3.50 p.m. They said good night to him as they passed him at the door."

The Sergeant paused for effect; Gareth could see he had something special by the glint in his eye.

"One of the cleaner's heard Johnny go, Sir."

"What!"

"Yes, sir, the lady that does that corridor. She heard the door open and slam and someone walk quickly away. She thought that it was Moran. She turned to say good night, because he always says goodnight to her, but there was no one there. She thought he must be in one of his moods. The corridor turns there, just passed the door. He must have shot round quick to avoid her. It wasn't Moran, so it must have been our man. That's why the room wasn't cleaned, sir. He'd dropped the catch, so she couldn't get in.

Gareth was on his feet, now.

"And the time, man! Did she get the time?

"Yes, Sir." Said the sergeant smugly. She checked her watch because she thought he was early. It was 4.20 p.m. exactly.

14.

Blake was back at Mere Green. Mrs. Moran had identified the body at the City Mortuary and he had run her home. She had said little on the way there or back. There were no tears either, she had set her armour and steeled herself. She had leaned across to gently kiss her dead husband on the lips and made the sign of the cross over him. Then she surprised him.

"Have you called a priest?

"Err, No! Should we?"

"Yes! You should. He would want the last sacrament, the sacrament of the sick."

"Isn't it a little late for that?" asked Blake.

"No, not if you're a believer. It's never too late, and it's what he would want. I can phone the presbytery when I get home if you like? If you'll let him in.?"

"I'm sure we can arrange something." Blake looked across at the mortuary attendant who nodded silently.

"If you'll ring a priest we'll give him every facility."

"What about the burial?" She was gaining strength and purpose now. She was all he had, he was hers again. She would arrange everything.

"That will be up to the coroner." said Blake gently, but when the body is released it will be to you as next of kin." That seemed to satisfy her greatly. He would be hers completely in death if not in life.

He had completely forgotten Feeney until the desk sergeant reminded him that he was still sat in an interview room, tying up a constable.

"He's been there for over two hours," said the desk jockey with thinly disguised exasperation.

"Where's DC Singh, then?"

"He's upstairs viewing that CCTV tape he brought in." The phone rang and he picked it up to give a monotone response. "Mere Green Police!" He hand the phone to Blake, "Your governor."

"Blake?"

"Sir."

"Give Feeney a quick once over and bring him back here. I want him to walk the building with us. We found the holdall and the statue, but not in the bin he was burning. He doesn't know that. Make him uncomfortable. Shake the tree and see what falls, then bring him back here, O.K?"

"Yes, Sir."

Kevin was distressed. He had been up since six a.m. He had missed his lunch. He had missed his afternoon siesta. He had been given the third degree by that sergeant, and the events of the day had just been overwhelming. Now he had sat for two hours in a police station "to help with enquiries" and nobody had spoken to him. His emotions were in bits. He was frightened and angry and upset.

Blake entered the room and sat down in front of him. He caught the constable's eye and gestured for him to sit at the table. He was still wearing his outside overcoat and had his hands in his pockets.

He crossed his legs and lounged back a little in the chair looking intently at Feeney. After a few seconds, which seemed like an eternity he leaned forward and picked up one of the two blank tapes lying on the table. He undid the sealed wrapping, placed it in the machine, repeated the process with the second tape and switched the machine on. Talking to the machine he intoned his message very slowly, "Interview with Mr. Kevin Feeney, caretaker of St. Norbert's Roman Catholic School, those present Mr. Kevin Feeney, Detective Sergeant Blake and Constable?," he looked at the officer enquiringly, "Hanlon, Sir."

To Kevin he said, "Mr. Feeney this is an interview under caution. You are not obliged to say anything, but anything you do say may be given in evidence. Do you understand the caution?"

Kevin's mind was in a spin. This could not be happening.

"You don't think I did it, do you?"

"Did you? Did you kill Michael Moran?"

"No! No, I couldn't kill anyone."

"You didn't like him though, did you? When you talk about him, you say Moran, not Mr. Moran. You always say Mr. Price when you mention the head and you said Mrs. Fraser about the lady teacher, but the dead man, he was just Moran. You didn't like him."

"No, I didn't like him. I don't like a lot of people but I don't go round killing them."

"We found the holdall, - and the murder weapon, - in the bins. Why were you trying to burn them?"

"I wasn't. I was burning the rubbish; --- to make space. We would have run out of space. I always burn the bins when the teachers over fill them."

Blake allowed a smile to play round his lips.

"You said the kids did it. You said they threw a match in the bins --- for kicks!"

"I know, I always say that. It's not allowed, burning the bins. The refuse company get shirty about it because they say it damages the bins. It only takes the paint off. How can you damage a big thick metal bin? I tell them that to save trouble, so they don't charge us for new bins. We really need more bins, but Moran won't pay for them. So when they're filling up too quick I burn them."

"Is there any thing else you want to tell me, about the bag or the statue, or anything else for that matter? Now would be a good time before things get anymore serious." He leaned forward slightly, staring fixedly to emphasise his words.

Kevin was very agitated now. "Look I don't know anything about the bag or the statue. I didn't know they were in the bin. It just looked like papers to me, and I didn't kill anyone."

Blake decided that there was no point in continuing, he had nothing to pressure with. Best leave it for another time when they would know more maybe.

"Well, as it happens, they weren't in your bin, not the one you burnt, so I believe you, for the moment. The Inspector wants us back at the school. We'll go in my car."

Edwards met them on the steps outside the front entrance at 5.30.

"Walk with me." He led them round to the back of the building and across the playground to the other side. They stood outside the door with the partially repaired wall and the scattered sand.

"Now this is where Johnny entered the building. It was after 3.50 and before 4.20 p.m. who would have been about at that time? He looked hard at Feeney. "Who had reason to be here?"

"Lots of people. Some of the kids hang around playing football after school."

"In the Rain?" Gareth interrupted. "It was raining."

"That doesn't bother 'em. They get soaked sometimes. They're barmy."

"But then they go home don't they? – not back into school?"

"They have to come this way or use the door at the other end. When school closes we lock all the exterior doors except this one and the front door and the one at the other end of the building by the kitchens. We lock all the perimeter gates too except the front entrance. After three-thirty the only way in from the playground is this one or the one by the kitchens, and the only way out is through the front door. It's a matter of security. We get a lot of intruders here if we're not careful. Some of the staff coming from the other blocks might have come this way. Music, Technology, the Inclusion unit, anyone coming from them would have to cross the playground to get into the main building. "

"Who does that, locks the gates and doors? You?" Kevin nodded at Gareth. "And did you do it last night, lock all the gates and doors?" Kevin nodded again and murmured "Yes, but I was late yesterday. A kid was sick in the boy's toilets and I had to clear it up. It would have been nearer to four when I locked up."

"So our man comes in this way," he walked through the wet sandy soil and in on to the corridor with the others trailing behind him, "from the playground, leaving his footprints all the way to Moran's office. Now the cleaner doesn't see him come so that must be before she gets here. What time do the cleaners start work?"

"Four o'clock," Kevin was still shaken by his interview and didn't offer anything further.

"So our man is already inside at four if she is on time. She presumably cleans up the footprints in the corridor after she's done the classrooms. Open the door."

Edwards handed over the keys to Kevin and waited for him to turn the locks and open up the room to their view. The surfaces, walls and floor shimmered with a silvery glow as the light hit them. Everything was covered with aluminium powder from the evidence gathering process. The outline of the head was visible on the computer keyboard, etched in blood and the rest of the body outlined on the desk and floor in chalk. All three looked around the room.

"He stands behind Moran," continued Edwards, "and has an up and a downer with him. He loses it, picks up the statue and hits him. Moran dies. Why doesn't he just leave the statue where he found it? Why take the bag? Perhaps there is something else in there that he needs. Anyway he drops the statue in the bag, opens the door, drops the catch and slams it behind him. He makes a bee line for the corner. He's round it before the cleaner turns and she doesn't see him. She can't get in now. So the footprints in the office stay."

As he gave his commentary he carried out each of the actions that he had described. He stopped just around the corner and looked at them and then down the long corridor that ran the length of the building. There was no-one to be seen and it was eerily silent. A door slammed in a side corridor some way down.

"Have I missed anything so far?"

They shook both their heads but said nothing.

"He's vulnerable now isn't he? It's early. Normally, there are still people about. Would there be a cleaner on this corridor?

"Three or four" answered Kevin; he was intrigued now by the process and felt involved in the investigation. His stress was subsiding and he wanted to help, to be co-operative.

"Doris does the staff room and the staff toilets and some of the offices in the middle there. Betty does this end of the corridor and the classrooms off it. At the far end is Liz, she does the classrooms and the corridor going right to the Gym, and Mary does the kids toilets and the corridor to the left including the assembly hall. They'd all be on or off the main corridor at different times. They all have rubbish bags with them. When the bags are full they take them down the main corridor turn left and go out the door at the end to the bins by the kitchens. There is a door in the middle by the stairs but I would have already locked that. He had to go past all of 'em. "

"Then there's the staff as well." added Blake. They would be using the stairs at each end of the building and the stairs in the middle to travel between their classrooms upstairs and the staffroom. They all end up on the main corridor at some stage, whether they are collecting tea to take upstairs or bags and coats to leave. Everybody has to use this corridor. Our man must have been seen by several people. If he was unusual or stood out they would have noticed. That should be in the statements when we get to them."

"He's staff isn't he?" Gareth put his hands in his pocket and leaned back against the wall. "He's not an outsider. He knows the building. He knows the routine. The people know him. He can move around without calling attention to himself. Last night was different though. He's upset, he's not normal, not his usual self and he's carrying a bag that doesn't belong to him, one that might be recognised by someone else. Why take that risk? Why not leave it in the office?"

"Perhaps he's panicking," said Kevin joining in the spirit of the re-construction. "Perhaps he doesn't know what he's doing. Perhaps he's just trying to get away."

"Or he wants to create confusion," Blake added. "He's hidden the weapon in the bag. If he can get rid of it, it might be more difficult to connect him to it. His prints might be on it if he hasn't had time to wipe them. He wouldn't want to mess with it there. It's bloody. If he gets too much on him it might be noticeable. People might ask him about it as he walks down the corridor."

"Isn't he going to have blood on him anyway," persisted Kevin, "after bashing Moran's head in?"

"Not necessarily," answered Blake. "The doctor said most of the bleeding was internal. The stuff on the keyboard was seepage from the scalp. The statue smashed right in. It would have acted as a plug; he might have picked up a bit as he pulled it out, a small spray, but not necessarily enough to be noticeable. It depends what he was wearing as well doesn't it?

"Right, follow me." Gareth strode off down the corridor and stopped just past the middle. To his left was the staffroom door, to his right the admin corridor with the management offices and the reception area, leading to the main door.

"He goes the full length of the building and out into the playground again, and drops the bag in a waste bin. Why not go straight out the front? If he's panicking he would take the shortest route out wouldn't he?"

"Maybe he has to go on," said Blake. "There are things he needs. His car keys, his bag? His classroom is down that end or out in one of the other blocks, and maybe he changes. He needs his shoes. If he's the joker who threw the trainers in the bushes by the gate, then he changes into his shoes."

Gareth was forming his picture of his opponent now. "He's cool, he's not panicking, but this is not planned. He didn't bring a weapon. He just grabbed whatever was available and lashed out. He probably didn't mean to kill. He's got to be very upset but he's in control. Who could change without it being unusual? P.E. staff presumably?"

"Could be loads of people," said Kevin. Lots of staff help out with sports with the kids and there are staff clubs, basketball and badminton. They don't have to be P.E. to use the facilities here, and then there's the kids. We have some big kids. It doesn't have to be a teacher does it?"

"No, I suppose it doesn't" said Gareth thoughtfully, looking down at Kevin's trainers.

"Come on." He set off again down the corridor talking as he went. "He comes back into the building, because he has to, to get out again. But where did he go first. He has to go out at the end here."

They walked down past the kitchens and dining hall and turned the corner. They stood once again by the bins. It was bitter. They shivered as they stood surveying the scene in the biting cold.

"So, why doesn't he drop Moran's bag in one of these bins? Why go on into the playground and put it in a waste bin."

"Well, you don't know which bin he put it in, do you?" Kevin wrapped his arms around his body as if to protect himself from the temperature. The other two were wearing overcoats while he was still in his old grey overall.

"He could have gone somewhere else first and put it in the bin on the way back. If he carries straight on he goes into the Technology block, there's six classrooms in there, and if he goes left and across the playground he gets to Music and Inclusion. They all have bins outside the doors and there's more bins around the playground."

"So, you emptied all the bins this morning and put the bags in the big bins."

"Yes, it's my daily routine."

"So there was nothing unusual?"

"No, it was just the same as every day."

"Right, time for a cup of tea, I think, I'm gagging. We'll go to your place, Mr. Feeney and we can have another little chat there can't we?

15.

The house was on site, just beyond the Tech. block. It was a small two bed-roomed detached house with the garage on the side. The house went with the job and represented a big saving on living expenses for the caretaker. It was warm inside and they settled round the table in a good sized homely kitchen. Kevin wondered whether they had the right to enter his house like this but he was too scared to ask. He put the kettle on and put three teabags in a large brown teapot. He took a milk jug from the fridge and put it on the table with a sugar bowl from the cupboard. He took 3 matching mugs from a line of hooks on the wall, each with its own mug. The walls were painted yellow and were bright and clean. The table had a blue, formica top and the chairs had seats of a matching colour. Everything was neat and tidy, nothing out of place. There was no clutter, no left over food, no ignored washing up, no crumbs on the imitation marble work surfaces. Mr. Feeney was a very ordered man. On a shelf were a line of cook books arranged by size in descending order and a family picture on a beach at the seaside. The man in the picture was a younger version of Feeney. Kevin shook a biscuit barrel onto a plate and placed the plate in front of them on the table. The whistle sounded on the kettle and he poured the boiling water in, stirred the pot and put that on a stand on the table as well, then he sat down opposite the two policemen.

Edwards smiled at him. It was a friendly open smile that put Kevin at his ease and made him feel a bit more comfortable.

"Your family?" said Edwards picking the photograph off the shelf and looking at intently. "Where was this taken?"

Kevin felt disconcerted again. It felt like an invasion of privacy for Edwards to pick up the photograph without asking and it irritated him.

"Western-Super-Mare," said Kevin. "Good times, when we were all still together."

Gareth put the picture back on the shelf.

"Where are they all now, then?"

"The eldest is in Spain, she's married to a solicitor over there. The wife died four years ago, breast cancer."

"I'm sorry to hear that Mr. Feeney, very sad."

Gareth's tone was compassionate, genuinely so. He and his wife had had a similar scare a while back but the tumour had turned out to be benign and had been removed safely. He remembered the fear of it. His concern reached Kevin and relaxed him a little.

"What about the younger girl? You didn't mention her."

"She's local; she works at the hospital; but we don't get on. I don't see her much."

"Why's that then?"

From anyone else the question might have been resented, but Gareth had always had a personal warmth which helped people to open up to him.

Nonetheless Kevin was visibly annoyed as he answered.

"She took up with an older man, a married man. We fell out about it and she stopped coming round. We're Catholics. I think it's one of the reasons I got the job. I told her it was wrong, but she wouldn't listen."

"Local man was he? Would we know him?"

Gareth could feel the tension rising in the older man and knew there was more to be said. He had touched a personal nerve. His instincts told him this was connected. Kevin had something to tell them that was eating him up. He could feel it in his bones.

"May I remind you, that you are still under caution, Mr. Feeney."

It was like a cup of cold water in Kevin's face. The two men looked at each other, each knowing that whatever it was had to be said.

"It was that bastard Moran."

What ever the two detectives were expecting it wasn't that and they looked at each other in astonishment. Kevin seemed to reduce back into his chair. He looked smaller and older now. His face was grey. The implications for himself were not lost on him.

"What our Mr. Moran," asked Blake in disbelief, "the dead man?"

Kevin paused, gathering his thoughts before answering. He knew he had just given himself a solid motive for killing Moran.

"After his wife left him, he started flirting. He chatted up the single women on the staff and went out with some of them. Understandable I suppose, but my girl was only half his age, and he was still married, and he used to teach her. Teachers shouldn't do that should they? They're in a privileged position. Both my kids went here and he taught them both. He met her in a pub and they started going out. He had plenty of money and a flash car and he turned her head. I supposed she was flattered. I knew she was seeing someone but she kept it secret, so I knew it wasn't right. He used to stop at her flat at weekends and eventually I heard about it. There's always someone wants to give you bad news. I was probably the last to hear. It was general knowledge before I knew, but I was told about it eventually. I went round there one Saturday and had a flaming row with both of them. Moran and I more or less came to blows and she threw me out. She asked me to go and told me not to come back. It was the worst moment of my life. "

He stopped. He was deflated, empty. He had said the thing that had been tormenting him all day since Moran had been found. He knew he would come under suspicion. He knew they would find out. In the end they had heard it from him, which was better than hearing it from the gossips. Blake broke into his silence.

"How old was your daughter when they started seeing each other?"

"She was twenty-two, just a kid."

"But old enough to decide for herself. He hadn't broken the law had he?

"Teachers have a way with kids, a special relationship. They shouldn't take advantage. It's not right, not with kids they've taught. He was old enough to be her dad."

"Reason enough to hate him then." said Blake.

"I hated him before that," said Kevin vehemently. The colour came back into his cheeks as his anger rose again.

"I used to be my own boss. I used to run this building. I am the Building Services Supervisor. When they made him Bursar they made him Site Manager. They put him over me after I'd done the job for 20 years without complaint. It was humiliating. If I was going to kill him I would have done it years ago. Anyway, it didn't last. After a few months he moved on. She told me he wanted her to get pregnant and she wouldn't. So he dropped her. Karen and I have never been close since though, the whole thing ruined our relationship."

He looked at Blake with obvious resentment. "Do you still think I did it?"

Gareth spoke before his subordinate had a chance to answer.

"We don't think anything like that at this stage, Mr. Feeney, but to be honest we wouldn't rule it out either. You see murder's not like any other crime. 95% of victims are killed by somebody close to them, a friend, a work colleague, a family member. Murder by a stranger is pretty rare. We know this murderer. One of us has probably seen and talked to him today. We just don't know who it is yet. It's a matter of relationships. Human relationships are very complex and we have to find out all about our Mr. Moran and his relationships. You are a part of the jigsaw, and a big one I grant you, but not the only one. I'm sorry if we've caused you distress. I'll be leaving a constable in the caravan in the car park over the weekend, but he won't bother you. If you can think of anything else that might be useful, tell him and he'll pass it on."

He stood up.

"Right, that will do for tonight. It's nearly seven. My people should all be finished by now and the building should be clear. Just one thing though,"

He took a plastic bag out of his overcoat pocket.

"I'll need those trainers and the cow gown for testing, just for elimination you understand."

Kevin took off his overall and his trainers and dropped them into the bag.

"Do you have a spare, by any chance? You know one to wash, one to wear that sort of thing?

Kevin nodded and fetched his spare overall from the cupboard under the stairs.

"You can do your rounds now and lock up. We shouldn't need to get in again until Monday."

Edwards and Blake walked back to the police van in silence. Moran was a complex character and could have given many people cause to desire his end, but what had pushed one individual into action. There was still a long way to go. They knew from past experience that they had to find the killer quickly. If they didn't have him within a week then it was likely to be months, or years, or never. As they got to the van Blake said, "You're Catholic, boss. What do you make of it? Moran's an intelligent man, but he has a funny sort of morality. Adultery's alright as long as she gets pregnant?"

"It's hardly in keeping with the teaching of the church. Most people take the bits of religion that suit them and reject those that don't in my opinion. Each individual makes up his own religion in the end, especially Moran. He may be intelligent, but he's not necessarily rational. He's obsessive about having kids. That's not his religion; it's his own personal hang up. Does a rational man destroy a good marriage because his wife is frightened of having kids? Why didn't they see a psychiatrist, adopt, or settle for each other? Lots of people do."

Sergeant Young and his constable were sat at the table in the van with the pile of statements that had been taken from the staff. Everyone else had gone.

"Evening, Sir. All done, for tonight then?"

"Just about, Sergeant, Just about, can you see that gets over to Highgate for testing." He dropped the plastic bag on the table.

"Have we got staff for the van?"

"Yes, Mere Green will have a man here on 8 hour rotation through until Tuesday morning. If you want any more than that, you'll need to bring in central staff. It's all our inspector will give you at the moment."

"That should be as much as we'll need. The van can go on Tuesday. It just gives a chance for anyone who saw anything locally to contact us at the weekend. Are these the statements?"

"Sir, forty-two teachers, 3 Secretaries, 2 lab assistants, one librarian and six cleaners, plus the ones you did yourselves. We didn't see any point in doing the cooks as they had all left the building before he was killed. I saw them myself and just asked if anything unusual had happened during the day. They didn't notice anything"

"You should still have got it in writing. Never mind we can pick them up later if we need to. Right! Blake, Statements, half each for you and me, bed time reading. Meet me at my place for breakfast at 8 sharp and we'll compare notes."

"At last! I thought you were going to let me down again!" Laura Edwards stood in the hall with her hands on her hips. She wore a neat black dress, matching gold necklace and bracelet, with a white knitted shawl. Her hair and make up were complete and she looked stunning.

"Have you forgotten we've having dinner with the Cheadles this evening?"

She didn't give him time to respond.

"Go on, upstairs, you've got 20 minutes to wash and change and then we're leaving. I'll phone and say we've been delayed. Hurry up."

He knew she would brook no opposition and hurried up to the bathroom obediently.

As they drove over to Walmley she chatted cheerfully giving him the outline of her day and then asked what he'd been up to. He gave her the bare bones of it. He disliked bringing the detail of his work into his family life. Much of it was grubby and best kept to himself. This case was different in that they both knew some of the characters in the play. Even their children had had some involvement. It touched on them personally, but the detail was still not to be shared even with Laura.

"Do you have any ideas, yet, as to who did it?

"It's much too early to be forming judgements. Let's forget about it and enjoy the evening."

"That's going to be difficult. John and Jenny's children are both pupils at St. Norbert's and Paul is in Mr. Moran's Maths class."

Gareth groaned inwardly, the last thing he needed was to be quizzed on the death, even by friends. Jenny and Laura worked together at the hospital as nurses on the same ward. He knew John from evenings like this and parish things. They had run the Irish coffee stall together at the summer fête.

He parked on the drive behind the family's car. The door opened before they reached it. They were expected and waited for. They were welcomed warmly and given sherry in the lounge. The whole family were present and they made small talk and laughed and politely no one mentioned the death of Michael Moran.

Gareth enjoyed his meal. Like Kevin Feeney he had missed his lunch, but he had been so busy he hadn't realised just how hungry he was until the hot winter soup, and bread rolls were laid before him on the table. The main course was Spaghetti Bolognaise with garlic bread. The wine was red and white Cabernet Sauvignon, red for him and white for Laura. She restricted herself to one glass and would drive home. The sweet was fruit and ice cream.

Gareth sat back with his coffee, relaxed and replete. This had been a most pleasant evening so far. The question he had expected came at last, from the boy Paul.

"I saw you in school today, are you investigating Mr. Moran?"

His parents shushed him and looked annoyed. "Paul! No! We said."

"It's alright." said Gareth, "the boy's bound to be curious. What did they tell you in school?"

"Not much. Mr Price said he'd died in school, and we said prayers for him, and he said we could have Monday off as a mark of respect. That's about all really, but it said on the news that it was suspicious and that the police were investigating it. I was in English and we saw the police caravan arrive, and all those other people. Was he murdered?"

"Paul! That's so rude!"

His mother was aghast. Gareth ignored her protestations. Might as well call a spade a spade, and there might be some mileage in this.

"It rather looks as though he was, but we'll have to wait for the pathologist to tell us for certain. You were in his class weren't you? What was he like?"

"Alright!" the boy shrugged his shoulders and then added, "Nobody liked him."

His father joined in, sounding annoyed whether it was at the boy's forwardness or his assessment of the teacher, Gareth couldn't tell.

"He got results though didn't he? You did well with him in SATS and he's entering most of your class for GCSE a year early."

"Yeah, but he used to blaze you, if you played up. The kids blaze each other all the time, but you don't expect the teachers to do it. It was alright if it was somebody else, because it could be very funny, but if it was you, he made you feel really bad in front of all your mates and they all laughed at you."

"He was sarcastic, is that what you mean." Asked Gareth?

"Yeah, he would say things to make you feel small, insults really, but he could be very funny."

"Well, I don't hold with that." said his dad, "Teachers shouldn't be sarcastic. Did he have a go at you?"

"No, I just did the work and kept quiet, so he left me alone. It was more the people who played up and didn't work. Some of the other teachers talk to you and discuss things. He was only interested in the work. That was all he was interested in, classwork and homework."

The rest of the evening passed pleasantly enough. The children went off to their rooms and their own occupations while the adults sat and chatted in the back lounge. The wives had much to talk about given their immediate everyday contact at work and went off into their own world of doctors and patients and hospital events. The two men had less in common. John Cheadle managed a Carpet Store and made a decent enough living supplying the needs of Birmingham households. They had some mutual acquaintances from church but not enough to make more than polite conversation and the turn of talk eventually turned back to Moran. Edwards the detective and Cheadle the concerned parent had one topic in common.

"Any ideas about who did it yet," asked John.

"Oh come on, John! Hardly, we only found him this morning; and if we had, I would have to be more circumspect than to respond to a question like that wouldn't I?"

"Yes, of course! Sorry. It's just that with Paul and Angela still being there, I don't like to think of a killer being loose with a connection to my kids. I hope there's not going to any other unpleasant events"

"This will all be over pretty quickly as far as the school is concerned. They don't have the time to sit contemplating their navels with 600 kids on site. Institutions shake themselves down and get back to normal in a week what ever happens. One or two individuals might be deeply affected, but the routine will push it to the back of most people's minds pretty quickly. Within six months the whole incident will be a faded memory whether we catch the perpetrator or not. I've seen it time and time again."

"Yes, and Paul doesn't sound that bothered. He might even be glad of the change of teacher by the sound of it, but I hope you get him. I still don't like the idea that it's someone who could end up in a classroom with my kids."

"Might be an intruder," reflected Edwards, "they have had a lot of problems in the past with that sort of thing, but not so much recently since they beefed up their security. They will probably have to look at that sort of thing again now. Anyway, time we were moving, it's going to be a busy day tomorrow. Thanks for the evening, it's been very relaxing."

On the way home through the darkened streets Gareth mulled over the days events knowing he would shortly have to read the witness statements that had been taken that afternoon. He had several conflicting views of Moran circulating in his head. There was Moran the charming younger man who was everybody's friend; the passionate lover adored by his wife; the talented teacher who rose to lead his own department in the difficult world of mathematics education. There was Moran the grumpy, morose older man; the estranged husband, the failed head of department, the sarcastic teacher who was disliked by his pupils. This change, apparently, being brought about by his obsession with having a child of his own. Then there was the Moran who was still so locked into his religious upbringing that he couldn't contemplate divorce but was able to totally disregard his church's laws on sex outside of marriage; and Moran the social animal who visited pubs where younger people hung out and still had enough charm to attract a young woman only half his age. Moran the bursar was still the man of power, with a controlling interest in the lives of the people with whom he worked for good or ill. The man was a jigsaw of contradictions. Somewhere along the line he had enraged another human being so much that they had ended him; and tomorrow he would have to try and find that person and ask him why?

Saturday 2nd. December:

16.

Blake arrived at 8 o'clock sharp as instructed and was met with the delicious smell of grilled bacon as Edwards opened the door.

"Just in time, I'm about to put the eggs on. Pour the tea will you? Laura's gone; she's on early turn."

Edwards busied himself at the stove while Blake got settled at the table and poured two mugs from the large teapot waiting there.

"Anything from the statements you had?

"Yes," Blake was stirring his mug thoughtfully and looking at his note book. "There were a number of people on that corridor between about 3.45 and 4.45, who saw each other and can vouch for each other so we can position them quite well.

Price went into the staffroom to pin a notice on the board and saw, Miss Summers and Miss. Wright talking to Mr. Hennessey. They saw him. He went back to his office and saw Mrs Hailey coming in through the main door. She'd been out on a course and was coming back to pick up exercise books. She went to the staff room for a cup of tea. She saw him and the other three in the staff room. As she walked down the corridor she saw Mr. Jarvis coming from Moran's end. He had been doing football practice with some kids and was in tracksuit and trainers. That's confirmed in his statement. He saw Moran go into his office at about 3.50 as he passed by, and that's confirmed by Mr.

Turner who saw them both while going in the opposite direction to talk to the music teacher. So Moran was definitely alive at 3.50. It goes on like that until they all leave the building. I've got a list of 8 people who might have been on the corridor between 4.15 and 4.30. They might have seen our man, or they might have been our man."

"Mine were much the same; I have a list of 11. We'll amalgamate the lists and maybe re-interview some of those today. Was there anything unusual?"

Blake shook his head as Edwards put the plates of bacon and eggs on the table. They continued to chat as they ate.

"Anything on the PM yet?" asked Edwards.

"Yes," replied Blake in between mouthfuls, "I rang the mortuary early on. They did it last night. The same pathologist is on duty today and will see us if we go up there later this morning."

"What about forensics?"

"Nothing, they're a bit pressed and haven't started on our stuff yet. They say we can have that spare set of house keys though, if we send someone to collect them. I left a message at Mere Green for Singh to pop into Gooch Street and pick them up when he gets in. I thought we might have a look at the CCTV video for the relevant times. He went through it yesterday while he was waiting with Feeney so he should know it pretty well by now."

"Good. That puts us ahead a bit. We'll do the Mortuary first, then the video, then the house. Then we can sit down and decide where we're going to make house calls. We've still got a wide open field to mow. More tea?"

He offered the pot to Blake's mug, but passed when Blake shook his head and went on to fill his own.

"I'll just set my video, Harlequins are playing this afternoon and I don't suppose I'll get a chance to watch the match. We'll take your car. You need the petrol expenses more than I do."

The Birmingham City Mortuary is a large, Victorian, red brick building just behind the Coroner's Court off Steelhouse Lane. They have full facilities to deal with all the post mortem examinations needed by the City's several hospitals. Murder victims are also stored there until the body is released by the coroner. Blake and Edwards swept into the City on the Expressway, a huge seven lane motorway with a central reversible lane. The central red lane is part of the route into the city in the morning rush hour and becomes part of the route out in the evening rush hour. The necessary changes have so far not resulted in any head on collisions in over 30 years of operation. It is connected to all the major motorways via the internationally famous Gravely Hill Interchange, known locally as Spaghetti Junction. Any unsuspecting stranger making a wrong turn there might have to travel 5 miles before he can find a way off to reverse his journey and correct his error.

They parked on double yellows outside the City's main police station in Steelhouse Lane, confident that the blue windscreen sticker would protect them from any roving traffic warden and walked round to the Mortuary building. The Victorian tiled floor sent echoes of their footsteps up to the vaulted ceilings giving an empty sepulchral feel to the place. It was a bit like being in church. They were directed by the receptionist to the second floor office of Doctor Warren.

"I've nothing much to add to the police surgeon's report. He was killed by a single blow to the head with a heavy object which penetrated both the skull and the brain disrupting cerebral function. He was a fit and healthy man in his forties. No evidence of disease. Heart in good condition, should have lived to a ripe old age but for one thing, which is very unusual and very unlucky."

He paused and looked over his report at the two police officers.

"He had a thin skull, just where he was hit. That part of the skull is usually rather thick and very strong. Most people would have probably survived the blow, with some damage, fractured skull, concussion etc. It would still have been serious but they would probably have lived. This chap could have fallen over, hit his head and killed himself at anytime during the last forty odd years. It was an event waiting to happen."

"But it was still that deliberate blow that killed him?" said Edwards

"Oh, yes, I don't think my report will do the defence much good. They might try to claim it as a contributory factor to get the charge reduced to manslaughter; but the fact is if he hadn't been hit he wouldn't have died, on this occasion at least. It's all there in the report. I've copied scaled pictures of the wound across to Gooch Street for comparison with the weapon. If there's any doubt they'll send it over here for direct comparison with the body, but I don't think that will be necessary. I think it's all pretty clear cut, inspector."

"What about time of death, doctor?"

"I would say Between 4 and 5 p.m. last night, given the temperature readings of the building and the state of the body."

"Ok, that tallies with the witness statements. Thanks for a speedy response. "

They arrived back at Mere Green police station just before 10 a.m... Hardeep was waiting for them in the not very spacious office they had been given as an incident room. He had a large white board set up on which to track the case but as yet nothing had been entered on it, also a television and a video player. There was only one desk, decorated with tea, coffee, milk and sugar, but he had acquired three straight back chairs for them and a kettle.

"Found anything interesting, then Singh?"

"Depends what you want to see, Sir. There are five cameras in operation and the recorder goes round them in sequence. It records about 30 seconds on each one in turn, so you don't have a continuous record. The cameras are all strategically placed to look for intruders going into the building out of hours. They sweep along the windows of the

building at vulnerable points on the ground floor,
except for one. That's focused on the main door
from the inside looking out so that the secretaries
can see who is at the door before releasing the
electronic lock to let them in. For our purposes
trying to find people in the normal course of
business, it's not much use at all. For example, on
the main door camera all you can see is the back of
their heads as they leave the building. Also they
didn't spend a lot of money on the system, and the
outside lighting is not very good in places, so the
quality of the tape is poor. If there is anything, it'll
have to be enhanced. There are a lot of comings and
goings but whether anything is useful or not, well I
don't know. It depends what else you have."

"Right," said Blake, "Our man enters the
building by the door leading to the English corridor
between 3.50 and 4 o'clock. He comes out of the
door by the kitchens at around 4.25 and goes into
the playground. He's wearing trainers and carrying
a medium sized, green holdall. He may go into one
of the other blocks. At some point he drops the bag
in a waste bin in the playground. He comes back
into the building by one of the two end doors, we
don't know which one, and he leaves by the front
door. He may have thrown a pair of trainers into the
bushes by the gate to the car park exit."

Hardeep moved over the beverages and rolled
out an A3 sheet on which he had a basic plan of the
school. He had already marked the camera
positions. He sketched out the route Blake had
described with a thin red pencil line. He had also

marked in the lines of sight of each camera and highlighted them in yellow.

"The camera on the Music block points at the side of the English classrooms and covers the door, but it's a dummy, just for show, completely useless. The camera by the kitchen door points at the Technology block and covers one side of it. We may have caught him there going into the block or the playground or returning from either. The one on the Technology block roof covers the Music and Inclusion Blocks and also about two thirds of the playground. That might be useful. The one on the main door should have the back of his head as he leaves. There is a camera pointing at the car park but it's another dummy."

"Why do they have dummies?" asked Edwards, "What's the point of that?"

"Cost probably," answered Hardeep, "It's just an empty case. It looks like the others but there's no camera inside. It can still act as a deterrent if it's highly visible, 'bit like some of our speed cameras. We do the same thing. Ok! Let's view the tape from 3.50 until 5.45. That's when Feeney locked the main door."

"Stop the tape!" Edwards stood up and peered at the screen.

They had been viewing for about 45 minutes when a dark figure carrying a holdall came into the view on the kitchen door camera. He was wearing a black hoody with the hood pulled over his head and was looking at the floor. The trousers were also black and gathered at the ankles. They might well have been track suit bottoms. The camera was looking at his back.

"I think that's him, isn't it? Go forward."

The tape moved on and the hooded man walked forward into the Technology Building. They waited for him to come out again with Hardeep doing quick bursts of fast forwards every few minutes. When the time on the tape showed 6.00 p.m. Edwards said in exasperation,

"Ok. Turn it off. We've missed him. Damn, damn, damn. Hardeep get that tape to the lab and ask them to isolate the bit we have got, and enhance it. I want A4 stills of the best bits. He must have come out while the tape was recording the other cameras."

"Well it was always a long shot," said Hardeep.

"Perhaps if we show that bit to the staff on Monday, someone might recognise him, or he might give himself up"

"All pigs fuelled and ready to fly." Blake yawned. "If that was my own mother I don't think I'd recognise her. Have you got the house keys that I asked for?"

"On the table over there."

"Right, drop the tape off and enjoy the rest of the weekend. Meet us at the school on Monday morning about 8.30."

When Singh had gone, they walked up to the canteen on the second floor for lunch.

"Your shout," said Edwards. "I did breakfast."

Over lunch they looked at their list of possible witnesses. Blake's eight and Edwards eleven contained several overlaps and they reduced it to a list 12 people who might have seen something even if they hadn't realised it at the time. All were on the corridor at some point between 4.20 and 5.45 on Thursday evening. All saw or were seen by at least one other person. No one noticed anything unusual.

"Let's start with the house, and then we can see a couple of these today, Yes?"

"Right, but not too many, Boss. I'd like to start the board before we knock off and I promised I wouldn't be late tonight. We're supposed to be going out."

"Policemen shouldn't make promises to their wives," chuckled Edwards. "Don't worry; I know what that's like. I've been in hot water enough times myself."

17.

Blake and Edwards pushed open the wooden gate to Moran's house again and again it creaked in protest. They walked up the leaf strewn path and noticed a twitching of curtains next door as they did so. Blake tried the latch key and this time it opened immediately. They stood in a dark sombre hallway lit only by the light from the door way behind them. When Blake closed it they were in semi-darkness even though it was mid afternoon and he had to scrabble around for the light switch. The doors to the rooms off were all shut. The wall paper was a dark floral green which was peeling in places and much in need of attention. There were cobwebs hanging from the ceiling. The carpet once a bright multicoloured pattern was dull and lifeless. An open wooden box hung on the back of the door behind the letter box and contained several envelopes. Blake removed them and put them in his pocket. They looked into the front room first. A television stood in the far corner and there were two easy chairs set on an Indian carpet square for viewing. The floor surrounding the carpet was bare floor boards. The current fashion for imitation wood laminate had not been exercised here. There was a coffee table in the middle with one of those large conversation piece books opened at a page with a picture of a tiger roaring. Along one side of the room ran a large built-in bookcase which was empty, but for the phone. Edwards lifted the handset and pressed the play button on the answer machine. The first message was from Elspeth, angry and abusive. She had made the call on Thursday evening after she had returned from the restaurant, thinking he had let her down intentionally. There were also three messages from the headmaster Price. All three messages simply asked him to get in touch.

They moved to the back room. The curtains were drawn and again they put on the lights. Most of the room was taken up with a large pine table with eight pine chairs around it. It had a bowl of plastic flowers as a centre piece There was a welsh dresser on the back wall with a nice collection of plates for show. The drawers contain cutlery and in the cupboard at the bottom was a collection of glassware. A reproduction of The Haywain by Constable hung on the chimney breast which jutted out into the room.

In the kitchen were all the usual furnishings, everything neat and in its place, but for a dish, spoon and mug in the sink. The dish showed remnants of cornflakes. When Blake opened the fridge there was a half empty bottle of stale milk. That was all. The cupboards contained an assortment of condiments, jams and marmalades and the packet of cornflakes, plus a few tins of beans and soup, but for the most part they too were empty. The kitchen door led out to a utility room with a washing machine and a tumble drier. The washing machine was empty but the tumble drier contained three shirts. A basket on top held a small collection of socks and underwear. From the utility room a door led out into the garden. The grass had stopped growing but it had not been cut in the autumn and was much too long. It looked more like a field than a lawn. There was a shed locked with a rusty pad lock for which they had no key. They could see a few tools and pieces of wood and other bric-a-brac through the window.

They looked at each other and Edwards shook his head. Upstairs each room had a carpet, a bed, a wardrobe and a chair. None looked as though they had been used in recent time.

"So where is he, then?" said Edwards.

"Sir?"

"Where is he? He obviously isn't here. We are talking about a middle aged man. Where are his books, his CD's, his videos, last Sunday's paper, and his clothes for that matter? He can't have lived on beans and corn flakes. What did he have for supper on Wednesday night? He's a teacher for God's sake, Where's his computer. Don't they all use computers these days? He hasn't been here for months has he?"

"No, Sir, maybe even longer than that. This isn't a home. It's an accommodation address. Maybe his post will tell us something"

They went down stairs and sat at the polished pine table in the dining room.

"He obviously cared about this, didn't he? Polished, no dust, it must have been done recently," said Edwards.

Blake slit the first envelope with a knife from the kitchen.

"It's a letter from his bank, sir, telling him that he's exceeded his overdraft limit of £1200. They may refuse payments if he doesn't make a payment in to bring it back into line." He slit the second envelope.

"Credit card Company. He missed his payment last month. They are telling him not to use the card until he makes a payment. They want £450. He owes £4730. His credit limit is £4500." He slit the third envelope.

"This one's from his Building Society thanking him for his business and asking if he'd like to insure his property with them."

"I thought he'd paid his mortgage off. That's what Mrs. Moran said wasn't it? The mortgage was paid up. Anything else?"

Blake slit the rest of the letters open and discarded each as he took in its contents.

"The rest is just junk mail, sir. These are the only three of any significance."

He handed them over to Edwards.

"So he had money troubles, our Mr. Moran. He couldn't meet his bills. Interesting for someone in a sensitive job like that eh. School Bursar, Director of Finance? I bet he wouldn't want his headmaster to know about that now would he? You get on to this Building Society first thing on Monday, Blake. We want to know about his mortgage and you'd better get a copy of the latest missing persons report."

"Missing persons, Sir?"

"Yes, Missing Persons, if he doesn't live here, he must be living somewhere else, mustn't he.

Someone may have missed him by now and maybe they've reported it. Let's get back to the office. We'll do the board together and call it a day. We need to think this out a bit more before we ask any more damn silly questions. We'll get everything we know on the board and I'll see you Monday at the school about 10.30. I'll go meet Singh at 8.30 and we'll show the whole staff the tape and see what's what. You get the Misper report and see the Building Society manager first.

Sunday 3rd December:

18.

"The Mass is ended, go in peace to love and serve the Lord."

Edwards crossed himself as the priest gave the final blessing. He stood through the last hymn without singing. He had found it difficult to concentrate as his mind was still on the events surrounding the death of Michael Moran. It had crossed his mind that Moran would be brought here for his funeral when the body was finally released and that he would probably be conducted to the cemetery by the same priest who was saying Mass this morning.

He was on his own today as Laura was again on the early roster. He had driven her to the hospital before coming to St. Francis' to fulfil his Sunday obligation; an obligation which he was not always able to meet because of the demands of his work. He joined the line of congregation edging slowly down the central aisle towards the exit; chatting amongst themselves as they waited to reach and shake the hand of the priest as they left. Fr. Michael liked to greet each parishioner personally at the end of the service, which made the exit as slow as a supermarket till queue. There were several of the school staff in the congregation and by the sideways looks he was getting, quite a few parents who obviously knew who he was, even if he didn't know them. He felt a light touch on his shoulder and half turned to find Mr. Price immediately behind.

"Good morning Inspector."

Edwards acknowledge the greeting with a smile and a nod and quietly mouthed, "Morning," in return.

"I wonder if we could have a chat today," Price enquired politely, "Something has come to light which I feel you ought to know about. It may concern your investigation."

"I'll wait by my car," replied Gareth. He had planned to go into the office to look at the board and review the statements a little later on but other than that, this was to be a thinking day. The prospect of new and unexpected information was welcome. Price extricated himself from the throng of people who wanted to "have a word with him" and joined Edwards at the other side of the car park.

"I can't tell them anything, but people are concerned," said Price, "It's understandable. Look this is too public here, could you follow me down to my place, it's not far and there is something I need to show you."

The rain had stopped but it was a dull morning with the promise of more rain later The Prices lived in a quiet road off the main street, which was probably quite beautiful in the summer when the trees lining the road were decked with leaves. At this time of year, their stark skeletons reaching up to the sky were sombre and a little depressing.

Price led him into a smart and well appointed study, much like his office at school only a little smaller. Mrs. Price enquired after their needs and went off to make them tea and toast. Price took an A4 manila folder from his desk and laid it on the coffee table between them.

"Just before this unfortunate business arose I had a visit from a city finance officer who told me that the school had been persistently robbed over a period of many months. In all about £33,000 pounds is missing."

"I take it this was not burglary or direct theft."

"No, Inspector. I believe it's what they call white collar crime, a fraud in fact. Somebody has been ordering goods in the school's name and then diverting them elsewhere and working a computer scam to cover the transactions. It's a nasty business as it puts a number of people under suspicion, including me. The police would obviously be involved eventually, but Miss. Bailey, that's the finance officer, left me to conduct my own investigation, we are to meet again on Tuesday. This is a file of invoices which the city has identified as being part of the fraud. It is not particularly informative in itself. The various goods were delivered to the school in holiday periods and at weekends, Saturdays mostly, and then taken elsewhere."

"Wouldn't your caretaker have been aware of these deliveries?

"You'd have thought so, but someone has been very clever. The deliveries were all arranged to take place when Mr. Feeney was away, either on annual leave or at weekends. I've checked the dates. I spent part of yesterday in school, once I got past your constable, checking for these goods. He wasn't happy about me being there, but he came with me and was very helpful. None of the goods ordered are on the school premises. We checked the serial numbers of anything that might have qualified. There's nothing. They're all gone. The only common factor is that all the delivery notes were signed by Mr. Moran. That's not unusual. He would be one of the people who would sign such notes, but all the items on the suspect list were received by him and by him alone. Someone else could have organised this theft but people hold different bits of knowledge and have different accesses to the building and the computer system. It would have required two or three people to collude. I know my people and I can't see that happening. The more I think about it, the surer I become, the only person with sufficient, knowledge, access and organisational skills to pull this off was Michael Moran. He would be able to do it all by himself. No-one else could. He has to be the obvious suspect. I would have had to confront him about this tomorrow but for his untimely demise."

Edwards picked up the file and started to read through it in his thorough fashion. Mrs. Price brought in the tea and hot buttered toast and Price helped himself. Edwards continued to read ignoring them. Finally he closed the file and dropped it on to the floor beside his chair.

"Someone has been setting up house, hasn't he?"

"I'm glad you're going to be looking into this, Inspector."

Mrs. Price was stood by the door watching for his reaction.

"Gerald hasn't slept for two nights worrying, what with this and the other business. I urged him to see you this morning. He wasn't sure that he should."

"No, you definitely should have told me and the sooner the better. In fact you should have told me on Friday but no matter, we know now. I wonder could you leave us Mrs. Price. There are things we need to say to each other."

"Yes, of course. I'll boil the kettle and keep it hot in case you need another pot."

"How did he get the goods off site? He would have had to hire a van for some of this stuff."

"He has a van. He used to show dogs. He bought a large white van to travel round the country on the show circuit. I believe he still has it."

"The next question is where did he take it all? Not to his own house that's for sure, I was in it yesterday. None of this gear is in there."

"Exactly and none of this is going to be easy to prove unless we can recover some of the goods and link them to him. However he has slipped up just once. He made a mistake. One item was damaged in delivery and returned to the supplier, he gave them a new delivery address to send the replacement to. He forgot to remove it from the paperwork. I have it here."

He held out a Copy Return form printed in Red on letter headed paper for a video recorder. The delivery address was handwritten in, and it was not Moran's official address.

"It is his handwriting. It's unmistakeable." said Price.

"Obviously I have no authority. I can't just call up there and ask to see the video, even supposing there is anybody there. However in view of your ongoing investigation, I thought you might want to take this on board as well."

"Well, I can't ignore it. It's convenient though isn't it? If a couple of your staff had been at it and knew they'd been rumbled, it would be a good opportunity to off-load the blame onto the deceased. I'm not a great believer in co-incidences. However that doesn't explain this address on this docket in his handwriting, if it is his handwriting. I will need to find out if it impinges on my investigation in anyway. If not I'll pass the file on to the fraud squad and ask them to contact you and your finance officer. Ok?" He picked up the file from the floor and stood up to go.

"I'll hang on to this for the time being."

"Yes, of course, but there's more. If you could bear with me Inspector, this is difficult for me. Matters of confidence are involved."

Gareth dropped back into the chair and waited for him to start again.

"It is difficult, as you will no doubt appreciate when you become party to information about staff privately."

Gareth nodded but didn't speak. The door swung open and Mrs. Price entered with another teapot.

"You must be ready for a fresh cup, I won't disturb you I'll just change these."

She swapped over the pots and closed the door again behind herself.

"Sorry about that," said Price.

"No matter." Gareth smiled and waited again.

I had a conversation with John Gerard, my Head of Technology on Friday afternoon. I had been trying to arrange a meeting with him in the morning but events over took us. When we finally did get together it came out that Moran has been pressurising him for money. He caused a deficit on a school trip account and Moran wanted him to make it good out of his own pocket. Complete nonsense, of course, I'm not happy with the deficit, but these things happen. It's certainly not the personal responsibility of the staff member concerned and Moran knew that. I can't understand what he thought he was doing. The amount involved was £700."

Price hurried on. He wanted to get everything off his chest in one go.

"Also earlier in the day I had a conversation with Miss Summers. Moran had also been putting pressure on her. She has had to have time off school and he had been stopping her pay. That might arguably be correct, though I would disagree in these particular circumstances. In any case it is well outside his brief. He would have no right to do that without my approval in any circumstances. She wouldn't necessarily know that of course and was greatly upset. There may be other examples of this sort of thing that I don't know about."

"Perhaps he was trying to fill the hole in the accounts before the audit." suggested Gareth.

"The amounts are too small surely. He would have to find a lot of transactions at this level to cover £33,000."

"Well there's only one way to find out something like that, "said Gareth. "You're going to have to ask the staff if he has been pressurising anyone else, aren't you?

19.

Gareth decided to go home first and have a think. He had been to the parish mass at ten and it was now nearly twelve. He sat in his kitchen and waited for his microwave meal to go ping. The address on the delivery docket given to him by Price would have to be checked. There would be little point in wasting time trying to get a warrant to search for stolen goods at Sunday lunch time. Even if he could find a co-operative magistrate it wasn't his main area of interest. He just wanted to know how it connected to Moran's death, if it did connect to Moran's death. He decided a social call was in order. He could make up some pretext for calling and just check out the scene. He would need to wait a bit. Let them have lunch and call over about mid afternoon to see what's what. He carried his Beef Lasagne into the lounge on a tray and sat eating it slowly with a knife and spoon. With a working wife micro meals were a god-send. He wasn't much of a cook and couldn't be bothered anyway. Something quick and filling and easy to do was all he required. He would eat properly tonight when Laura got home. He watched the television news and got himself a coffee from the kitchen. Then he dozed off for a while in the chair. He had always had the ability to fall asleep almost anywhere and anytime. It was a useful technique on long drives when they were on holiday. He would pull in to a service station. Sleep for 15 minutes and wake up completely refreshed to carry on with the journey. He awoke at 1.30 and had a wash to freshen up and then left to carry out his plan.

The address was a small estate of maisonettes on the eastern edge of the City near the border with Solihull. 603 Creswell Road. It was a two storey block with four residences upstairs and four down. The block was surrounded by a communal lawn but there was a small drive on the left leading to a parking area and a communal set of washing lines at the back. Beyond these were eight garages which formed the back boundary of the property. All the doors to the houses and the garages were painted in identical royal blue. No.603 was on the ground floor in the middle. The kitchen was to the left of the door, and the frosted glass told him that the toilet and bathroom was to right, followed by a small bedroom. There was no net at this window and as he walked down the path he observed a cot and a pram in the small bedroom. The lounge and main bedroom would be on the other side of the building. Nice starter homes, thought Gareth, Just what every young couple would want. He rang the bell.

The door was answered by a beautiful afro-Caribbean girl in her late twenties. She wore bright yellow shorts and flip-flops and was bare legged. She also wore an extra large purple tea-shirt and was heavily pregnant.

"Hello?" Her smile was like sunshine on that dull dreary day and her voice musical. Gareth felt quite cheered by the whole picture. He held up his I.D. making sure that his photograph and the city police emblem were clearly visible, but with his finger over the word inspector.

"Constable Edwards, on enquiries madam. I wonder if I could speak to Mr. Moran. I believe he lives here."

"Andy, what do you want with him?" she was a little apprehensive now.

"Oh! Nothing serious madam, just paper work and red tape. May I come in?"

She ushered him into the lounge at the back of the property and he sat on the easy chair of a three piece suite whose description he had read earlier that day on a school invoice. The television, he noticed, was the same make as one described on another invoice and he had made a note of the serial number in his notebook.

"Mr. Moran ran a red light a week or so ago. He was given a caution and asked to produce his driving documents at a police station within 5 days. He hasn't done so, so I'm doing a follow up. We don't like to leave these things."

"Oh, dear! He must have forgotten. He has been very busy. He's in Manchester. He's an Ofsted inspector and he's often away for a week or so at a time."

"But he does live, here madam? This was the address he gave."

"Well no! He has his own place but he spends time here. He's waiting for his divorce to come through and then we'll be getting married. They're going to sell the house and divide the proceeds as part of the divorce, and then he will move in here.

So, I suppose he does live here, really. This is his."
She tapped her tummy with both hands.

"I'll need the address his other place then, if
that's the address on his driving documents. Could I
have your name Madam, just for reference, you
understand?"

"I'm Katrina Harding. He's not going to be in
trouble is he?"

"Oh, No, madam, it's just paper work. And the
other address is?"

"45. Regal Road, it's in Erdington."

He made pretence of noting it down in his
notebook but he already had the confirmation he
was looking for.

"So you both live part time here and part time
there then, do you?"

"No, I don't go there. I wouldn't want to bump
into his wife she still owns half of it. It would be
awkward."

"You wouldn't have his driving licence and
insurance documents here would you? Then we can
get this cleared up right away."

"I don't think so, but he does keep some papers
in the dressing table in the bedroom. I'll just have a
quick look."

He waited until she reached the end of the hall
and he could hear her opening and closing drawers.
While she was out of the room, Gareth did a quick
sweep of the photographs around then room.
Michael Moran aged 46 stared back at him
challengingly everywhere. He was in swimming

trunks on the beach, with his arm around her in evening dress and walking hand in hand with her in woodland. He checked the serial number of the TV and the video. The TV matched one detailed by the auditor. The video was the same as the delivery docket he had been given by Mr Price. They both matched numbers he already had. He heard her close the bedroom door and sat down again.

"No, sorry! He must have them with him. I'm not expecting him back until next Friday, but I'll tell him if he rings. Can he present his papers in Manchester?"

"Yes, I'm sure that would be fine. "You say he's an inspector?"

"No, not really," she laughed, "he's an adviser for the city. He goes round schools advising teachers of mathematics, but he's part of the City's Ofsted team and they get hired out to other Education Authorities. He goes away four or five times a year. He likes to think he's an inspector, makes him feel posh." Her laughter was completely infectious and he joined in with her.

"Just one thing, you called him Andy. He gave his name as Michael Moran."

"Michael, John, Andrew Moran," she laughed again, "He prefers to be called Andy."

"It's a nice place you've got here."

"Yes, we like it. The flat's mine, but Andy bought all the furniture. It was bare when I was on my own. I could only just afford the mortgage."

"Right! I'll leave it at that then," said Gareth, "If you could just tell him to get in touch?" He shook hands with her at the door, and noticed that she held part of the weight at her front with her other had. Not long to go there, he thought. He smiled at her and turned away, but his face set hard as he walked down the path.

20.

The staff were gathered in the lecture theatre on the second floor of the Technology block at Edwards' request. It was where they normally held staff and other large group meetings. What was unusual was the presence of all the ancillary staff in the same group, secretaries, lab assistants, the librarian and also Kevin Feeney. There was a low rumble of chatter as he entered with Mr. Price and stood at the front. DC Singh had set up the tape in a video player which was hooked up to the ceiling projector. He had also obtained and set up an overhead projector next to it and was already sitting at the side of the machine. Mr Price introduced him.

"This is Detective Inspector Edwards of the Murder Investigation Unit. He is in charge of the investigation into the death of Michael Moran. He would like to talk to you all. Inspector!"

"Good Morning. I'm sorry to be meeting you under these circumstances. Some of you already know me as a parent, as both my children went to this school. I'd like to thank you all for your co-operation so far. Mr. Moran was your colleague and it must be very distressing for you, but we do need your help. Mr. Moran was murdered on Thursday evening between 3.50 and 4.20 p.m. We are pretty certain of those times from the interviews that we conducted on Friday. He was seen by various people and we have at least one witness who was aware of the killer leaving his office."

There was a gasp when he said this.

"Unfortunately the person concerned didn't see his face and couldn't identify him. However we think he was caught on one of your CCTV cameras. We would like you to watch this short clip and see if you can see anything that might help us. DC Singh."

Hardeep nodded to the technician who turned out the lights and then he started the tape and the screen burst into light. The enhancement had improved the lighting conditions and every thing appeared to be much brighter than they had been in the original tape. The contrast was better too. There was a clear view of the windows of the technology. block as the camera swept down the side of the building to the gap between its corner wall and the main block. As it slowly returned a dark hooded figure moved forward carrying a holdall and entered the main door of the block. The scene was repeated three times. On the second showing Hardeep spoke to them.

"Look carefully please. That holdall is definitely green and we think it is Mr. Moran's missing holdall. The person is wearing a dark blue or black hooded track suit. We thought it was black on the original tape, but it looks more like blue on the enhancement. It has a white stripe down the one leg; maybe down both but we can't see the other one. Do you recognise that track suit? Do you know anyone who has one like it?"

On the third pass of the camera he directed them to the man himself.

"Look at the shape of the man, or woman, we don't know which. Average height, five foot six, five foot seven, maybe five foot eight. Average build not fat. Look at the way they're walking. Does that remind you of anybody?

The lights went up and the buzz of chatter started again.

"Well," said Hardeep hopefully, "Anybody, anything?"

Nobody answered. People looked round to see if anyone else had spotted anything, but nobody spoke. At last Derek Turner commented.

"To be honest, that could be anybody. There's nothing to get a handle on."

There was a murmur of agreement across the room.

"Ok, we'd like you to have a look at this please."

Hardeep had moved to the overhead projector and put up a slide showing an enlarged plan of the ground floor. Edwards took over the session again.

"We're fairly confident that the person that we are looking for left Mr. Moran's office here at 4.20 and walked the length of this corridor here, to go out by the kitchen door here, where he was picked up by that CCTV camera. The time on the film is 4.26 pm. From reading your statements we believe that twelve of you were on that corridor at about that time. They are Mr. Price, Mrs Lamb, Mr. Turner, Miss Summers, Miss. Wright, Mr. Hennessey, Mrs Hailey, Mr. Jarvis, Miss. Murphy,

Mrs. Parsons, Mr. McLaughlin and Miss. Kavanah. There were also four cleaners who may have been in the vicinity for a few moments at a time, Doris, Mary, Betty and Liz, but that's not certain. This person must have walked right past you. Think back; some of you were stood talking; some of you were walking to the staffroom, or from it; some of you were going to the main door to leave. Who passed you, who did you pass. Somebody must have noticed this person in a dark tracksuit carrying a green holdall."

Then staff looked around at each other and back at him. All looked completely mystified.

"I remember the people you've said but nobody else." The speaker was a small, dark haired young lady in her twenties with a strong Irish accent.

"You are?"

"Mary Kavanah, I was standing by the main stairs in the middle, talking to Eileen Murphy for about 10 minutes I could see the corridor both ways. I didn't see anybody else, just the people you've mentioned."

"Perhaps, he was invisible." said Edwards with irritation though he retained his big smile. This wasn't getting him anywhere.

"Some people are invisible." It was DC Singh that spoke.

"You don't see the people you expect to see, do you? How many of you notice the milkman or the postman walking down a road when you are driving to school. They are part of the street furniture, like a letter box or a telegraph pole. This person was there. They walked down your corridor. Who wouldn't you notice walking down your corridor because you would expect them to?"

There followed a pause which was so highly charged that Edwards could feel the tension rising in the room; then three or four people spoke at once.

"The cleaner, the relief cleaner, the guy with the mop and bucket."

Edwards stepped forward.

"Alright, one at a time please, and give me your names as you speak."

"Derek Turner, Deputy Head, there was a cleaner, with a mop and bucket and a black plastic rubbish bag, she walked past me just like you said. I just didn't think."

"Paul Jarvis, ICT teacher. He had a woolly hat; I thought it was a bloke. He was just the relief cleaner."

There was a murmur of argument as others disagreed. Edwards raised his hand to stop them joining in.

"What do you mean the relief cleaner?"

Mr. Price answered him.

"We don't actually employ the cleaners, Inspector. They are employed by the City through a department called City-Clean. If one of our cleaners is sick or can't work Kevin phones them and they send a relief. It happens quite often. We're all quite used to seeing different faces mopping or sweeping, or not seeing them as your colleague has just pointed out, and sometimes it is a man."

"There was no relief cleaner on Thursday night."

Kevin Feeney was standing at the back of the room by the door.

"I know because I would have made the booking. All my ladies were here that night. There was no relief cleaner."

The hubbub started again. Edward's had to call again for their attention.

"Right! Ok! Look! Can anyone who remembers having sight of this person stay behind, the rest of you can go about your business within the school but please stay available in case we need you again. I will want to re-interview a couple of you to check detail. Mr. Feeney would you please stay as well."

Mr. Price was by the door now, blocking the exit.

"Just a word before you go."

The conversation died and they turned and listened to him.

"You can all find plenty to do with in your departments, I'm sure, so I'll leave that to you. It has however come to light that some staff were, well there's no easy way to put this, being put under financial pressure by Mr. Moran. If this applies to you and you have not already seen me about it, could you please come to my office and discuss it with me. I won't say any more than that, but please be assured I am looking for answers, not people to blame. No matter what the circumstances are, come and see me. Thank you." He stood aside to let them leave.

Gareth and Hardeep took details down in writing of each person's memory of the unknown cleaner. It wasn't much. Between 4.20 and 4.25 an unknown person who may have been male or female, walked down the corridor carrying a mop and a bucket in one hand and a half full dustbin bag in the other. He or she walked past 12 people who thought it so normal, that the passer-by barely registered on their consciousness.

"Boy is he/she cool," observed Hardeep. "I don't think I could have walked down that corridor past all those people if I just bashed somebody's brains in."

"Cheeky, arrogant, even," replied Edwards. "He knows the building. He knows the routine. He knows the people. The idea of being caught isn't registering at all in his mind."

"Or she," added Hardeep.

"I'll stick with he for now, if you don't mind, until I have reason to think differently. Most of that lot expect a cleaner to be female. It's stereotyping. Smashing skulls with heavy objects is a male sort of crime."

"Who's stereotyping now," chuckled Hardeep?

"Alright, Alright, Smart Alec! Well done, there by the way! We nearly missed that. You pushed the right buttons for them. What about the equipment Mr. Feeney? Where did he get the mop and bucket?"

"The cleaners don't have their own," said Kevin, "there's half a dozen in the cupboard under the stairs. "They get one when they need it. If there's one out and they need it they might just pick it up and use it. I'm guessing that Ivy saw those foot prints and fetched one. She would sweep first before mopping, they always do. If she found it gone she would just presume someone else had nabbed it and fetched another; same with the plastic bag."

"He put the holdall in the rubbish bag to navigate the corridor didn't he? Hardeep was trying to reconstruct the perpetrator's thoughts.

"He knew someone might recognise it so he needed to hide it. He can't be staff, or even recent staff. sir. People would have recognised him as out of context. He got away with it because they saw him as a complete stranger, doing what a stranger should be doing; but where did he get all his information?"

There was a tap on the door and Paul Jarvis came in.

"Look this might be completely stupid!" he stopped not knowing whether to go on or not.

"We'll tell you if it is, man. Just say it."

"Well Mike Moran used to help out with badminton after school sometimes, and he had a dark blue track suit with a white stripe down the leg." Edwards jumped up as though he had been stung.

"He used Moran's own track suit to hide in. That's why he needed the holdall. He put some of his own clothes in the holdall."

21.

Blake sat in his car outside the building society waiting for them to draw up the blinds and turn the closed notice to open. He had been there since eight forty-five and watched the staff go in, in ones and twos. It was a largish high street branch and had about 10 staff. He read bits of his paper and absent mindedly watched the business world go by. He had Moran's letter from them in his pocket with the cyclostyled signature of M. Carlyle, Manager. It was probably a form letter. They opened up At 9.30 a.m. on the dot. He locked the car and walked into the branch and up to the counter. He held his warrant card up to the protective glass window.

"Detective Sergeant Blake to see Mr. Carlyle please, he is not expecting me."

He always loved the effect that had. The startled girl went swiftly to the back office and returned to invite him through the door at the side of the counter.

He was shown into the usual bank style office. It looked empty, unlived in, depersonalised. These offices were just like interview rooms really. The real private office was further back and the public would never be invited that far into their world.

Mr. Carlyle wore a light grey business suit and gold rimmed glasses he was slightly balding at the front but tonsorially well endowed at the back and sides. He looked more like Blake's idea of a university professor than a bank manager. The people who saw him about his overdraft were always younger, go getting types, with a keen eye on their interest rates. Blake held out his warrant card again for him to see clearly.

"Sergeant, I presume this is official as you've used your I.D.?

"Yes, Sir." Blake passed him over the letter he found in Moran's letter box and sat back while he read it."

"Just a standard letter, we send these out to all new customers. Is there a problem?"

"I am investigating the death of Mr. Michael Moran. He was murdered last Thursday evening. I need to know about his dealings with your company. We understood that his account was paid and closed. You said he was a new customer?"

"Ah! He's that Mr. Moran! I saw the report on the news and in the local paper on Saturday. I'll need to go and get his file." He left the room leaving Blake to look round at the advertising posters on the wall. He returned directly with a thick double sided manila folder.

"Yes, you're right."

He was reading from the file, not giving information which he knew himself.

"Mr. and Mrs. Moran took out a 20 year mortgage in 1979 and finished repaying it in 1999. However they didn't close the account. They left £50 owing to keep it open. A lot of customers do that. It means we continue to store the deeds of the property for them and they are able to continue their house insurance with us at favourable rates."

"So why the letter?"

"Didn't his wife tell you? They re-mortgaged to buy a holiday home earlier this year. We still insure their current property, but we were rather hoping to pick up the insurance on the new property as well. There's a note here saying they wanted to buy a cottage in Lincolnshire. We valued their old property at £180,000. It was a bit run down. It would probably fetch £200,000 if they did it up a bit. They borrowed another £120,000 over 20 years. They're both in the 40's with good jobs, so there was no problem with that. They have life insurance on the loan payable on first death. Everything is paid up and in order, so this account will be closed when Mrs. Moran makes the appropriate application and presents the death certificate."

Blake looked at him long and hard.

"Did they both sign the papers on the second loan?"

"Oh yes! That would be necessary of course. It's joint ownership."

"And did she come into the office to do so?"

"I really can't answer that, Sergeant, I wouldn't have dealt with the transaction personally, but they are old and valued customers. It could all have been dealt with by post. Why do you ask?" Blake ignored the question and moved on.

"Did you handle the new purchase?"

"No, it was a cash deal, no further mortgaging was required. We paid a cheque into Mr. Moran's bank account. Is there a problem?"

"Mrs. Moran may not be aware that she has a second mortgage. She and Mr. Moran split up three years ago. She moved out of the matrimonial home and now lives elsewhere. She did not seem to be aware of any of this when we spoke to her."

It was Mr Carlyle's turn to sit back.

"I see. In that case I am not sure what the position is. I would have to take advice from head office. Off the top of my head, if he has forged her signature and she is the innocent party, our insurance division might still pay out, but they would probably want to try and recover the original loan, in either cash or kind. I don't know. I am going to have to refer this one upstairs. In the mean time I'll cancel the direct debit and mark the account as 'no further payment required.' I'll need a copy of the death certificate in due course?"

"That won't be available until after the inquest."

"No, of course not, but I'd better write to Mrs. Moran and ask her to come and see me about these matters. Can you give me her current address?"

"Not yet." Said Blake. "There's the matter of confidentiality and we will need to verify all our facts first. We will inform her in due course and advise her to contact you."

Blake's mobile sounded off just as he was getting back into his car. It was the Forensic Lab in Highgate. They had something for him. He drove straight into the city without reporting to Edwards first. He thought he might as well get as much information as he could before checking in. He rounded the Central Fire Station and cut right across the traffic and sped round into the backstreets to avoid the traffic round St. Martin's. He cut across Digbeth to make his way down Sherlock Street and into the lab car park in Gooch Street. He presented his credentials at Reception on the first floor. He was shown into another interview room much like the one he had left in the building society branch. The wait was longer this time. They were used to detective sergeants and didn't rush about for them. Eventually a young blonde lady in the obligatory white lab coat appeared.

"Morning, Miss Birchell."

"Good morning, Sergeant Blake."

They had had dealings before and knew each other quite well.

"I wasn't expecting such a quick response; we know how busy you are."

"Well, yes we are; and this is not a full report, there is still a lot to do; but something came up that I thought you might want to know about straight away. The statue had blood on it, mostly on the front corner of the plinth and we matched that to the victim. Then we sprayed the whole thing with Luminol just in case."

"Luminol?"

"Yes, it's a new technique we're trying, from the States. It's a chemical that fluoresces when it comes into contact with the iron in blood cells, and bingo we got a result. There's a small residual blood stain underneath the statue just here. She took the bagged statue out of the box she had carried in with her and pointed to the dog's underbelly."

"Is that important?" asked Blake.

"Well, yes! Because it's not his! This statue was made in a mould of some sort before it was attached to the plinth and it was made upside down. This mark here is where the funnel would have been to pour the molten metal into the mould. It's been cut off and filed but they didn't do a very good job and it's left a sharp and rough bit just there. When your killer picked up the statue and hit him, he cut his finger on it. Probably the second or third finger on the inside. The victim was blood group O. This is A-negative. I don't have enough residues for a good DNA match, but if you have a suspect with A-neg. blood and a cut on the inside of his finger it might help."

"That's it.?"

"That's it. We may have more for you later in the week."

Blake rang Edwards on his mobile at five to eleven and they arranged to meet to update each other. They all arrived back at Mere Green Police station at roughly the same time. They sat and compared notes and got the details up on the board. When they had each finished, they sat in silence for a while. The mortgage fraud, the deceived wife, the young girlfriend heavy with child yet full of hope and expectation, the dalliance with the caretaker's daughter, the theft of school assets; all these things weighed heavy on the three men.

"You know I am getting to thoroughly dislike our Mr. Moran," said Edwards, "In fact if he wasn't dead already I might be tempted to do the job myself."

"Ditto," said Blake.

"So where to next?" joined in Singh. "We can always congratulate his killer, but we have to catch him first." The two older men both burst out laughing.

"Well done Hardeep, you're good in this firm; I think we might want to keep you." Edwards stood up and became serious again.

"We're nowhere are we? We have plenty of motives among the innocent, no obvious suspects who might be guilty. Let's hope forensics can come up with something more useful later on. Hardeep and I will go back to the school. There are two more interviews I want to do, and you can go and ask everybody their blood group Hardeep. Donating is the sort thing they all get encouraged to do at college. They've probably all done it at least once so you should get most of them. It won't necessarily help, but no stone unturned as they say. Blake, chase up that missing persons report and meet us back there.

22.

Christine Summers sat opposite him in the deputy head's office. She had taught history at St. Norbert's for the last 13 years.

"Is this about the cleaner? I didn't really see her; she just passed me, that's all."

"No, I think we're fairly straight about that." Edwards opened his note book and checked some of the information he had previously obtained for this interview from Price.

"You are one of the longer serving staff and you've been here since you were probationary teacher." She nodded.

"So you'd know Mr. Moran very well. I'm still trying to build a complete picture of him in my mind. You know, to help me think why someone might have wanted to do this to him." She nodded again and there were tears in her eyes.

"Well you probably know him better than many of the other staff; tell me what he was like."

"He was a marvellous man. Charming, considerate, funny. He always made you feel good when you were with him. When he talked to you, you felt as though there was no-one else in the world that was more important to him. Just you."

Edwards sat back in his chair in complete amazement. According to Price this woman had been put under severe financial pressure by Moran and insulted by him in public. He had even told her to put her mother in a home. Now she was singing his praises like a sweetheart. Suddenly he twigged.

He dropped his pencil and note book on the table and stood up. He walked round table and leaned thoughtfully against the wall with his hands in his pockets.

"You were in love with him."

"We had a relationship, yes." She sat with her legs crossed and her hands clasped in her lap. She stared back boldly at him.

"When was this?"

"We finished it at half term, in October. We went out for about eighteen months and one thing led to another. We were lovers. He was the most marvellous gentle lover."

"So why did it end?"

"Because of mother, he didn't like her and she couldn't stand him. He wanted us to move in together and be a family. He wanted a child. His first wife couldn't have children. I couldn't leave mother. He said he would look after me if I got pregnant. He said there would be no problem with financial security. I wanted to, but I couldn't with mother there. I asked him to wait because she is dying, but he got exasperated."

"What about him stopping your wages?"

"He didn't want to. It was his job as bursar. He said it would look like favouritism if he didn't."

"So why did you, go to Mr. Price, last Friday?" She looked at him angrily with colour rising in her cheeks.

"Yes he did tell me. He had to. In view of what happened he had to tell me everything about Mr. Moran. You understand." She nodded and went on.

"I was upset. I had some big bills that week. I told Mike and he was angry. He said if I put mother in a home and moved in with him he would take care of the bills and I wouldn't have to worry. He still wanted to have a child with me. He said it because he loved me, but I couldn't, not with mother the way she is. I thought Mr. Price might be able to help. Mike was only saying those things because he was expected to. It was his job."

"Right, well I think that's about it, Miss. Summers. Thank you for your frankness. It has helped me get a few things in perspective. I have a much better picture of Mr. Moran in my mind now. Would you ask Mr. Gerard to come in, please?" He watched her. How could a man like Moran inspire such loyalty in women? It was completely ridiculous. How could they believe him? Perhaps it was just because they wanted to believe him.

John Gerard came in and sat down abruptly. He was a pleasant faced man, but looked as though he was simmering. He sat with his arms joined on his belly, one leg crossed over the other with the ankle resting on the knee and he swung over on the chair's back legs, just balancing with his one foot on the ground. There was defiance in his eyes. Before Edwards could speak he said.

"I didn't kill Moran for seven hundred quid."

"I never thought you did, Mr. Gerard, never thought you did. But he was putting you under financial pressure wasn't he? Why was that?"

"To punish me. I broke his rules. You could have a deficit on an account providing you went and crawled to him first. If he didn't agree it up front, it was a mortal sin."

"Well, you put it a bit strongly, but isn't that just good financial practice. It's the way the banks work. Overdrafts are agreed up front?"

"Nobody loses money on purpose. It was a cock up and I was responsible, agreed, but Moran wasn't interested in solving the problem. I had sinned and I had to be punished. That was how he operated. He was going to try and make me make up the loss. I wasn't having it and told him so."

"That's why you argued," he looked at his notes, last Tuesday evening?"

"Yes. I saw Mr. Price about it and he agreed with me."

"That was on Friday after Mr. Moran's body was discovered."

"Yes, I had tried to see him earlier, but Moran got in the way of that too." The comment brought a smile to Edward's lips.

"Yes, he wasn't very co-operative, was he? Mr. Turner said that he was generally obstructive with you lot, the heads of department? That right?"

Gerard nodded.

"Tell me about it. Who did he upset and why?"

"Just about anybody that wanted to bring about change in this place. You can't change things without money. He controlled the money. The only chance you'd got was to get him on your side first. If you could do that you were home and dry. For example we had a very good Head of Modern language here for a while. We have a lot of ethnic minority kids and they speak a variety of community languages. The kids don't really want to do French anymore and don't choose it in the options in the upper school. She wanted to bring in peripatetic teachers and introduce Punjabi, Vietnamese, Chinese and Hindi as GCSE subjects. He argued there wasn't enough call for each language to justify the cost putting it on the curriculum. She left and we have French teachers teaching other subjects because there isn't enough work for them to do. That was a fairly typical example of Moran in action."

"What about Mr. Turner didn't he support the idea?"

"Derek! No he just wants a quiet life. He wouldn't go up against Moran."

So who among the present Heads of Department has he upset or blocked recently?

"Everybody and nobody is all I can tell you. He upset just about everybody one way or the other, but nobody would want to kill him for it. You don't kill somebody because he doesn't agree with you at work. I don't know what Moran was into but for someone to do that it must have been personal. It can't just have been work. That's silly. Isn't it?"

"O.K. Mr Gerard I don't think I need to ask you anything else. Thanks for your time."

Edwards walked out to the police van in the car park. Hardeep was already there with a brew on.

"You were right, Boss." He had heard Blake call Edwards "Boss" and was emulating him. It sounded cool.

"They all knew their blood groups except for Mr. Price. He was the only one who had never given blood. They're nearly all group O. There's only one group A, Mrs Frazer and she's not negative. So that eliminates all of them doesn't it?

Edwards didn't respond. He was still mesmerised by the two interviews he had just conducted. He sat there and shook his head in disbelief especially at the gullibility of Christine Summers. Finally he said,

"You know what, Hardeep? I'm coming to the conclusion that Moran was as nutty as a fruit cake."

Blake bounced into the trailer, breathlessly and dropped a file on the table. He had run from his car in his determination to transmit his information as quickly as possible, but his exertions made it difficult for him to speak. Hardeep made him a cup of tea to his taste, milk two sugars, while he brought his breathing under control.

"You are not going to believe this, Boss. We've got another one! The computer had a likely missing Persons report made at Stetchford Police station on Saturday morning. John Moran, aged 46, didn't come home on Thursday night and has not returned since. I decide to go over and get the file rather than wait for them to send us a copy in the internal post. The Report was made by his partner, a Miss Joan Canfield. The description fits. She spent all day

Friday waiting, phoning friends and checking hospitals in case of an accident. When he didn't come home on Friday night either, she decided to report it. She handed in a photograph as well. It's him! It's our Michael Moran!"

Before anyone could respond, a small elderly black man stepped into the van. His check sports jacket was buttoned against the cold and a flat cap was jammed tightly on his head. He had a large scarf wound round his face and lower jaw against the weather and an open fronted transparent plastic Mac hanging from his shoulders and was accompanied by a multi-coloured terrier type dog on a piece of string. His eyes flickered round the room trying to decide who was in charge.

"Good afternoon, Gentlemen. I saw your notice on the fence about wanting information. Is this the right place?"

Edwards stood up and pushed his chair towards him. "Yes, of course. Would you like tea, Hardeep! Tea for Mr. ---?"

"Johnson, Errol Johnson, and no tea. I don't drink the stuff. I'll have coffee if you have some, black, and no sugar."

He laughed showing a full set of brilliantly white teeth. The others smiled in acknowledgement.

"You wanted to know if anyone saw anything unusual on Thursday night. Well I did. I saw something very unusual."

The three police officers were all ears. This was the first off site and independent information they had had. Possibly worth more than the statements of all the connected witnesses, anyone of whom might be lying. Hardeep poured water into his coffee and passed it to him.

"I walk my dog three times a day, morning, noon and evening. I go up the drive there by the side of the school, through the broken fence at the top into the park and I come back the same way. I don't usually see anyone up there because there's not a proper gate and not many people know that the fence is broken."

He smiled his big smile again."

"Well on Thursday night I was coming back through the fence and I saw someone come over the railing into the dive just at the back of the school, carrying a plastic sack. I stood still and shushed the dog. I don't like to meet people in the dark by myself like that. This person stood there and took off their trousers. I couldn't believe my eyes. I could see the white legs reflected in the school lights. Then she puts on a skirt, it was a woman! It was a long skirt, nearly down to her ankles. Then she changes her shoes and goes off down the drive. As she passed the end of the drive she threw something into the bushes. She gets into a car parked on the road and drives away. Isn't that something unusual?" Edwards responded with enthusiasm.

"Yes it is. Mr. Johnson. Very unusual and very helpful. You may have just solved a mystery for us. Just one thing though. Are you sure it was a woman? One hundred percent sure?"

"Oh, yes, definitely a woman. When she walked down the drive she was swinging her hips like a woman. Men don't walk like that."

"That's really useful, Mr. Johnson. That's a big help. Look I've got to go now, but what I'd like you to do is stay here with Constable Singh and go through it again with him, and he'll get it all down in writing. See if you can remember anything about the car, make, size colour, a bit of the number, anything alright?

"Easy man, the dog likes the warmth in here, he's lazy. I have to make him do his walks to stop him getting stiff." His laughter filled the van.

"Blake!" Edwards beckoned him outside. "We're going to Stetchford."

23.

The Berrow Lane house was number 67. It was an Edwardian three story town house set back from the road with a neatly fenced brick block drive. The house had full double glazing which looked new and the woodwork sealing the roof beneath the tiles was freshly painted. On the drive were a white Peugeot Boxer van and a Citroen Saxo saloon car. Edwards tried the keys from Moran's bag in the lock. The second Yale fitted. He dropped them back in pocket and rang the bell. The door was answered by a young white woman of about 30 years of age. Edwards was immediately struck by her looks. Her shoulder length hair was Jet black and shiny and she had fine symmetrical facial features. They showed their warrant cards and introduced themselves and were invited in. Her face was tear-stained, she was obviously very upset. The house was beautifully furnished with good quality furniture much of it new looking. There were framed photographs of the girl and a child on the wall and on the mantel. All had Moran in them as well.

"Thank you for coming, the desk sergeant didn't seem to think there was much that you could do other than record him as missing. He's never been missing before. When he's away he always phones everyday."

"Excuse me," said Edwards, "just for the record, you understand, you're not married are you?"

"Not officially, if that's what you mean, but as good as."

"Mr. Moran lives here?"

"Yes, with me and Jodie. We've been together for about two and half years. We had a flat for a while then he bought this place for us last summer. We had been seeing each other before his wife left him though. Then we had Jodie, she's just two."

"I gather Mr. Moran is away a lot."

"Yes, but never out of contact. He teaches Maths and he does Outdoor Pursuits. You know, walking, camping, canoeing, residential courses with the kids. He has to go away quite a bit, but I knew that before we got together. He always keeps in touch when he's away. Something must have happened to him. It's been 4 days now. I worried a bit on Friday and rang round everybody we knew and the hospitals. I even rang the school but they just had an answer phone on saying they were closed until Tuesday, so I didn't know what to think. He doesn't like me doing that. He likes to keep home and work separate. Then on Saturday I went down the police station to report him missing."

"You've never been there then? To the school I mean?" asked Gareth. She shook her head.

"No, he doesn't go to staff dos. He says they're very boring. People just talk about work. I don't think he likes some of them very much."

"What's he been like recently? Any money problems or other worries, a bit depressed perhaps?

"What, John! No, he's never depressed. He's always happy and laughing and joking. He loves to play with Jodie and take her for walks in her buggy. He's a brilliant dad." She was close to breaking into tears and turned to the box of tissues beside her.

"Excuse me. I'm just so worried about him." Then she cried. They waited for her to calm herself. Edwards had made up his mind.

"Have you been listening to the news reports since Thursday?" She looked at him blankly.

"No we don't have a telly. John thinks it dulls the mind. We both like radio and we play CD's and talk and go for walks."

He was sure this was the man and this was where he lived. He knew the next bit was going to be extremely difficult. She turned away from him again to sob into her handkerchief. Gareth mouthed "WPC" to Blake and pointed at his mobile. Blake stepped out into the hall and closed the door.

"Do you have any friends or relatives nearby who we could call?" asked Edwards.

"I'll be alright now." She broke off as she realised the significance of his words and stared at him, wide eyed with fear.

"You know something don't you?" There was never a good way to do this in Gareth's experience. You just had to do it as gently as possible.

"We have found a body, Miss. Canfield and we believe it is Mr. Moran. I'm very sorry."

Now she burst into floods of tears and hugged a cushion to her face in despair. Suddenly she dropped the cushion and fled the room, running blindly upstairs to a bedroom on the first floor. Edwards followed behind her. She gathered up a child from a cot and hugged it to her breast and continued to cry. The child awoken suddenly by her mother and made fearful by the noise of her mother's grief started to cry as well. Blake joined them and whispered "on her way boss."

Later, downstairs, Joan, still clutching her child sat on the couch next to the WPC. Edwards and Blake sat on the fireside chairs. She was calmer now but still so very upset. She had managed eventually to give Blake the number of her sister's place of work. The sister had been phoned and was coming. While they waited sipping fresh cups of tea, Edwards was thinking of another girl over in the east of the city with whom he would eventually have to do this again. At this moment he genuinely hated Michael John Andrew Moran, as much as it was possible for one human being to hate another.

"Are you sure it's him." She asked suddenly. "You might have made a mistake."

"I'm fairly certain. We got identification from someone who knew him well on Friday."

"On Friday? So why didn't you come and tell me then? How did he die?" There was anger showing in her eyes now. He could see her thoughts in her face. 'He should not have waited this long. She had been through hell. Someone should have come to her.' She was ready to fly at him now and there was no way to assuage her with kind words. The truth, the facts had to be told. Lies wouldn't do. There had been quite enough lies one way or another. He really didn't want to add to her burdens now but she was challenging him and it could not be avoided.

"Miss Canfield, this is going to come as bit of a shock to you. Mr. Moran appears to have been living something of a double life. He had another address, and we really didn't know about you at all until your missing persons report came over to Mere Green this afternoon. I'm sorry I can't give you much detail at the moment, but I have to tell you that the man you know as John Moran was also known elsewhere as Andrew Moran and elsewhere again as Michael Moran. He had three different addresses to go with those three names. I also have to tell you that Mr. Moran was in fact murdered on Thursday evening" She was wide eyed with disbelief now, and shaking her head in denial. Then she fainted.

24.

They drove back to the school in silence. Both men were hardened by the many human tragedies they came across in their work, but they had both been deeply affected by the young woman's distress in these circumstances. They also both knew that there was worse to come when the full story was finally told to everyone concerned. Several people's lives would be adversely affected for ever because of the obsessive nature of Michael John Andrew Moran. Hardeep brewed up again in the police van while Edwards read over Errol Johnson' statement. He passed it over to Blake.

"We're getting closer, but we're still no where near, are we."

"We now know it was a woman," said Hardeep.

"Do we?" Blake handed the statement form back to Hardeep.

"How about a cleaver disguise or a transvestite?"

"No, I don't go with that," said Edwards. "That old man has been appreciating women for a lot more decades than you or me. I'd put money on it that he knows a lady's walk when he sees it. It also fits other facts doesn't it? Why take the holdall from the office? Why not just leave it? If you're wearing trousers you can put a track suit on over the top, but a skirt would be all bunched up round the waist wouldn't it? No, the lady is wearing a skirt, it comes off and goes in the bag, and so do the shoes. She picks up the mop and bucket and when she gets round the corner she drops the holdall in the cleaner's plastic bag. I bet when we get the Forensic report that those trainers in the bushes were Moran's too. She used his gear to escape from the building into the technology block. She wasn't on the video coming out, because she never came out. Not the front anyway, she went out the back."

"So how did she get out?" Blake raised the obvious counter. "Feeney had already locked the other doors. Did she have a key?"

"She had his school keys in the bag, but she didn't need them," said Hardeep. "It's been too long since you two were at school. Sensitive or dangerous areas, with chemicals or machinery can be locked to prevent entry, but not to prevent exit. It's Health and Safety regs. People have to be able to get out. All the doors would have quick release bars on their locks on the inside in a Tech Block."

Edwards sighed.

"You're right we are too old. That passed me by. We are definitely going to have to talk to somebody about keeping you. So then she transfers her clothes to the plastic bag and drops the holdall in a waste bin in the playground. Again she misses the cameras because they don't cover the entire area. She goes over the fence, so she's young and fit. That fence is five foot high. She changes and walks away as if nothing had happened. We know what she did but we are no nearer to knowing who or why than we were last Friday afternoon, are we."

Blake tapped his finger on the table thoughtfully.

"But if it's a woman and if any of them knew about any of the others, that gives us four suspects doesn't? They would be his wife, Joan in Stetchford, his girlfriend in Tilecross and Miss Summers in school."

"And anyone of two dozen others that we don't know about." hissed Edwards. "The man was an obsessive philanderer. He could have girlfriends scattered all over Birmingham. No! None of those four could have scaled that fence. Elspeth's too old, Katrina's nine months gone, Christine's not fit enough and Joan would never leave her baby for long enough to do all that. We need to find something a lot more concrete. We're still up the river without a paddle. The only thing we do know is that she knows too much. She knows the site, the routine, the people and how everything works. No stranger off the street could just walk in and be lucky enough to do all that without prior knowledge. She knew Moran. She knew where his office was. She got there without being challenged and escaped elaborately so as not to arouse suspicion. I still think we're still looking for staff or ex-staff."

Hardeep stood up and moved towards the door. "If the blood group evidence is correct that lets out the present staff except for Mr. Price and if it's a woman that lets him out too. So ex-staff maybe? I'll go and ask the secretary for a list of everyone who has left in the last 12 months."

"No, hold it." Edwards pointed him back to his chair.

"In the first place, we only have their word for the blood groups; we'll need to check them later if we can narrow the field down. It will help if some one has lied but we don't have enough evidence to justify a mass testing. The same will apply to ex-staff. We can hardly go and say, 'you used to work at St. Norbert's and we think you may have killed someone, can we have a blood sample?' We need a reason to target them. In the second place, I'm going to need the secretary with me this afternoon. I'm going to have to give the bad news to Mrs. Moran and Mrs. Parsons seems to be the nearest thing she has to any sort of friend. You go and check out those doors in the Tech Block, and the fence and the drive. Follow the route. See if you can find anything OSG might have missed. Police work is attention to detail. I want this theory verified. When I see Mrs. Parsons I'll ask her to get together a list of leavers for tomorrow. Blake get in touch with Highgate again will you? Don't phone, go yourself. We really need some hard evidence from them. Go and see that nice Miss. Birchell you're so friendly with and tell her you're desperate." Blake broke into a huge smile.

"I have done, boss, but she just laughs at me."

25.

Gareth and Margaret Parsons arrived at Elspeth Moran's flat just after 1 p.m. The loud music was still playing from the downstairs flat and to Gareth's ear still sounded like the same piece of cacophony. She was elated to see Margaret Parsons again and greeted her warmly. She invited Edwards to sit in the lounge while she and Margaret went off to the kitchen to brew up and catch up. There were still photos of Michael Moran dotted around the place. Edwards wondered how such a man could inspire such devotion. One large photograph was now adorned with a piece of black ribbon. When they returned with tray and cups and all the paraphernalia of a Sunday afternoon tea party the two women continued to chat like long lost cousins. Edwards bided his time to wait for a suitable opening. She was still looking pale and drawn, but she had let down her hair from the bun and shed the glasses. She looked 10 years younger. Eventually there was a lull in the chatter and he found them both looking at him expectantly.

"I presume this isn't a social call, inspector." Elspeth was watching him intently now.

"No. I've asked Mrs. Parsons to come because I have some bad news to give you and I thought you might want a friend with you."

"That was thoughtful," said Elspeth, "but you could hardly be telling me anything worse than you did last time could you." Her voice trembled a little and he could see the death of Moran was still troubling her greatly.

"The fact is we have found out a lot about Mr. Moran during the last few days, which as his lawful wife will affect you. Mr Moran has had a number of liaisons with other women over the last three years and has fathered at least two children that we know of."

He could see the shock of his words on both their faces but he had to go on. She had to know; she had to deal with the consequences.

"He has not in fact been living at your former home for some time, just occasionally. He bought a house in Stetchford with money he obtained from re-mortgaging the property you jointly own, and he has a common law wife and child there."

"How could he do that? I own half the house. I never agreed! I never would have agreed!"

"We think he forged your signature. Obviously there are legal and financial implications for you in all this. The building society manager will be getting in touch with you shortly and will help you sort out the details. Legally you still own the house, he tells me, and Mr. Moran's life was insured with them which should cover the debt, but you will need to talk to him about that."

"What about this other woman? Does she know about me? Was she in it with him to forge my signature?"

"She knows very little at this stage, only what I've told her. I believe she is a totally innocent party and she is as upset as you are at his death. She just knows that she has lost her partner and the father of her child."

"Oh, poor woman, she must be devastated." Elspeth had a generous heart and her sympathy was genuine."

"I'm afraid there's more," said Gareth. "Your husband was also living on a part-time basis with another young woman in a maisonette in Tilecross."

He saw the open-mouthed disbelief spread over the faces of both women as he spoke.

"She is also pregnant and due to give birth any day now. She does know about you. He told her you were separated and getting divorced and that he would marry her when the divorce came through." Elspeth was beside her self now and sobbing; Margaret cradled her in her arms and patted her shoulder gently.

"Look I have to tell you these things, because both these women and their children may have some claim on his estate. I would advise you to get a solicitor as soon as possible. This is all going to get very complicated for the three of you."

He had warned Mrs. Parsons in the car that it was going to be difficult and that he would have to leave them and go on elsewhere. She mouthed at him, "no more," and gestured to the door.

"Right, well I'll leave you both, now. I have another call I must make. Perhaps when you have had time to digest all this we could talk again."

He made his way out by himself and sat in the car for a minute before driving on. They don't tell you much about this sort of thing when you're training, he thought, and it always drains you. You never get used to it. Perhaps it's just as well. Anyone unaffected by these things couldn't do the job anyway. He turned the key in the ignition and headed east for Tilecross.

26.

Gareth stopped in the car park of a public house about halfway there and rang the local station for assistance. He arranged to pick up a WPC on his way and started to steel himself again mentally for what would be another stressful and emotional meeting.

At Creswell Road the door was answered by a ginger haired girl who seemed very familiar to Gareth but he couldn't quite place her She was about he same age as Katrina and wore nurses' type uniform with a fob watch and a name plate which said she was Karen. She had a dark blue plaster on one of the fingers of her right hand which contrasted with the pale blue of her uniform. Edwards displayed his I.D. and they went through into the lounge where she introduced them. Katrina was relaxing on the sofa with her feet up and an aertex blanket over the lower half of her body. She showed surprise at the introduction, sat up and swung her feet round on to the floor with difficulty.

"Inspector Edwards, I thought you said you were a constable?"

"I apologise for the deception but I had to be sure that the Mr. Moran living here was the same Mr. Moran that I am investigating. I'm afraid I have some bad news for you. Could you tell me who this lady is please?

"This is Karen. She is a midwife and she is going to deliver my baby. She is also my friend from the hospital; we have known each other for years. I used to be a physiotherapist before I developed the bump." She smiled and ran her hands over her tummy."

Gareth had been dreading this particular interview since the previous afternoon when he knew he would have to conduct it. He had left it until last because every fibre of his being railed against the injustice of her situation, but now the time had come. He gave the information he had to impart as calmly and as plainly as he could, without elaboration or omission. She listened intently to him and sank back as his words assaulted her. She clung to the child inside her for comfort and was wrapped up in the arms of her friend as Elspeth had been before her. There was a long moment of silence when he finished. He could think of nothing further to say that wasn't lame and inadequate. Katrina clung to her friend and sobbed softly into her shoulder. Suddenly she sat bolt up right and clutched at her stomach. She let out a long low moan, then a painful scream. "It's started."

Karen was looking directly at him in a sort of daydream. She reacted immediately. "There's nothing more you can do here, Mr. Edwards. I'll take her to the hospital in my car it will be quicker than waiting for an ambulance. This was expected she is just a day or so early. It will be alright. Her case is in the hall, could you lift it into the car for me."

Edwards and the WPC, watched them drive off, then he gave her a lift back to the local station, before returning to St. Norbert's.

27.

Blake and Singh were not in the police van and the duty constable hadn't seen them since they had all left earlier in the afternoon. Darkness was creeping over the site again. Edwards wandered into the school, where he met the head and his two deputies talking earnestly in the foyer.

"Ah, Inspector! The staff are mostly gone; there was no one to ask so I presume that's alright? Edwards agreed; there was nothing further to be gained from them until they found another angle on the case.

"We have the children back in tomorrow, and we want things to be as normal as possible for them, you understand, despite everything."

"Of course," said Edwards. "The van will be gone from the car park tomorrow morning and we will be transferring our base to Mere Green Police Station. We'll leave the posters up for a few weeks to jog people's memory." The organisation was beginning to shake down. The horror and the shock had receded and the main priority was to get back to normal. Routine would take over on Tuesday morning.

"At some stage we are going to need to get at the finance computer in Mr. Moran's office." Price looked a little embarrassed, "We still have to prepare for audit and this time without a bursar."

"I'll have to block that for the time being. I want that room closed until I get the forensic report in case we have to recheck it. The rest of the school is yours again. You're meeting this finance person again tomorrow, aren't you?" He didn't wait for a reply.

"I'll need to see her with you. I have some information for you both. You may have to postpone the audit for a while. I don't think that will be a problem given the circumstances. Have you seen either of my officers, by the way?" It was Turner who responded to his question the others shook their heads.

"Mr. Singh was in Technology for a while then he met up with Mr. Feeney and went over to his house."

"Thanks I'll try over there."

When Kevin opened the door, he was beaming. The tension of the last three days had fallen from him. He was relaxed and happy and wearing a smile fit for a king.

"Ah! Inspector! Come on in the Kettle's on."

He went into the kitchen to sit with Singh at the table where he and Blake had conducted the interview on Friday evening. The tension of that evening was in stark contrast to the happy atmosphere that pervaded the place now. Hardeep stood as he entered but he waved him back to his seat.

"Mr. Feeney has been telling me about his family and showing me some pictures of his daughter in Spain."

"I'm going to move out there when I retire." said Feeney, "She's asked me to go and move in with them. They've got a big place and I can help with the grandchildren while they're both working." His face was suddenly serious.

"You know I'm so relieved you've eliminated us all in the school. Mr. Singh has been telling me that you're convinced it's an outsider and a woman. I was sure you thought it was me. I had visions of being locked up for ever. All this business, with Moran, you know, there's nothing left for me here now. I don't think I'm going to hang about. I'm 53 now. I can draw my pension in two years and they'll pay it over there. So that's me. I'll finish this year and go in July." He smiled again.

"You'll maybe miss your younger daughter, though" said Edwards, making conversation.

"Ah, well! That's it isn't! She came round last night and we had a long chat. She wanted to put things behind us and make a fresh start. We went out for a meal and it was just like old times." He chatted on merrily while he poured the tea and served them.

"She's always been very wilful that one; but she's a good hearted girl really. She gave us trouble right from the word go. She was a Rhesus baby."

Edwards was only half listening to him. There was something very definitely eating at him some thing he had missed. His eyes wandered around the kitchen taking in the décor and furnishings and coming finally to rest on the shelf with picture of Kevin and his family on the Beach at Weston Super Mare. Kevin was still talking.

"She's pretty fed up with the NHS, always short of facilities. She's talking about moving out to Spain as well. She should have no trouble getting a job with her qualifications."

Edwards' eyes were fixed on the picture of a little ginger haired girl holding her father's had on the beach at Weston Super Mare. The eyes and the mouth hadn't changed that much, in the picture she would have been about 12 years old.

"Your daughter works at the Hospital, doesn't she, Mr. Feeney? Is she a nurse then?" Edwards was almost holding his breathe now waiting for the answer he expected.

"Karen, oh no!" said Kevin proudly, She's a midwife."

Hardeep seemed unaware of the tension in Edwards and smiled and nodded and responded politely to each piece of information the old caretaker handed out.

"Do you know, I think I met her today, Mr. Feeny, over in Tilecross? I had to go there on other business. She was with a pregnant lady who was nearly due, a friend from the hospital."

The effect on Hardeep was electric. The smile left his face and his brow furrowed in concentration. Feeney didn't notice and continued.

"You mean Katrina, the physiotherapist. They've been friends for years, apart from when Moran had her in his clutches. He kept her to himself so she lost touch with all her friends. They've caught up again now though, and Katrina has a new man too. Karen's going to deliver the baby."

"I think she'd hurt her finger," said Edwards. "She was wearing a plaster. I couldn't help noticing because it was bright blue."

"Oh, Yes! They all have to wear those at the hospital. It's so it can be seen easily if it falls off. It's part of their infection control. Cooks have to wear them in restaurants too, in case one drops in the food."

"More tea?"

"Oh, No thank you Mr. Feeney. We have to be going. Things to do, you know, and you'll want to be making sure your cleaners are on task with the school re-opening tomorrow won't you?"

"Yes, indeed. I never thought I'd be glad to see the little blighters back, but it will be good to get back to normal again."

"Well, thanks very much for the tea; let's hope we don't have to bother you again."

He hurried out of the house and back to the van at a swift pace with Hardeep almost running behind him. Blake was waiting for them there. Hardeep was beside himself.

"The daughter?"

"Don't say anything." insisted Edwards.

"We're adjourning to the incident room at Mere Green, constable." He said to the duty officer in the van. "You can get us there if anything comes up alright?"

To the others he said simply, "Let's go."

28.

Edwards sat down at the table.

"First things first, Hardeep, kettle, three coffees, it may be a long night. What have you got Blake?"

His sergeant got out his notebook and started to read.

"There was a clear thumb print on the table by the coffee cups. It's recent and it doesn't match any of the school staff. They're running it through the National Data Base to try and find a match but they don't expect a result before tomorrow, that's presuming we do have it on file. That could belong to our mystery guest. The footprints in the office were not made by the trainers found by the gate. They were Moran's trainers so she probably lifted them from the office along with the tracksuit. They've managed a DNA match to Moran for those. If we can find the target's footwear we might get a match to the footprints. They got good impressions with singularities and they're size six. They lifted quite a few unidentified fibres from Moran's jacket that don't match his clothing but they could have come from people who were in and out of his office legitimately. If we can find our target and get her clothing then again they may help to confirm that she was in the room with him. That's it. If we find a target we can probably match them to the office, but what we've got isn't going to help us find her. The only chance is that thumb print."

Singh could contain himself no longer.

"But we have a target now! Bring her in and match her up."

Blake looked mystified, Edwards just shook his head. We have a suspect but we don't have enough to arrest her and test her. You can't just go around fingerprinting and DNA-ing the great British public on the off chance that you might get a result. No evidence, No arrest. No arrest, no fingerprints or DNA swabs unless the subject co-operates, and she's hardly likely to do that is she?"

He looked across at his sergeant.

"There have been some developments, Blake."

He started by giving them an account of his visits to Elspeth Moran and Katrina Harding.

"Now I had a feeling I'd seen the midwife before but couldn't place her. I didn't twig until I joined Hardeep here in Kevin's house and saw the photograph of the family again. She's Kevin's younger daughter. It appears that Mr. Feeney's daughter Karen knows Katrina Harding. In fact they are long term friends. Now Katrina may not know anything about Karen's affair with Moran because she went out of circulation while the heat was on, but Karen sure as hell knows all about Katrina's affair with him. His photograph is shouting at her from all the walls in the flat, and she is also the Midwife who is delivering the baby."

"Do you think they're in it together?" asked Blake.

"My gut feeling is, no. When I told Katrina about Elspeth and Joan and the other child, I thought she was genuinely dismayed and distressed.

She had no idea that she wasn't the only one in his life. I don't think she was faking it, and I don't think she was aware that Karen had been involved with Moran. Karen knows the school building and the set up because she was raised there. Karen is also wearing a plaster just where we might expect our lady to have cut herself on the dog statue. Our dear Kevin had a reunion with her last night and they mended fences. He was so happy about it that he was warbling like a blackbird and he happened to let drop that she was a rhesus baby. "

"What's the significance of that, Gov?" asked Hardeep.

"Well there you are then, you young people don't know everything do you? The Rhesus factor is contained in blood and may be negative or positive. If the parents have different signs then the baby can end up with the opposite factor to the mother. Now this doesn't normally affect the first born namely Karen's elder sister, but it does set up antibodies which can kill the second child, usually they have to give it a blood transfusion to save its life. Now if our Karen was a rhesus baby there's a fair chance she might be our "A negative" blood donor on the statue. All of which gets us precisely nowhere. It's back to good old fashion police work again.

Hardeep you're on the computer. First the National Police Computer, see if she has any sort of record, you never know we might already have her finger prints and DNA on file. Second the electoral register, UK info.com, 192.com or anywhere else you can think of, I want an address for her and I don't want to ask her dad for it."

"Why not just ask the hospital?" said Hardeep.

"Because they wouldn't give it me, Constable, Data Protection Act. Never ask for information unless you know your going to get the answer. The person you ask might alert your suspect. Now she may or may not know that we've made the connection but she will do as soon as she talks to her father again so we haven't got long.

Blake, you get a search warrant be ready to put an address on it as soon as we have one, and house a tame magistrate for the rest of the evening. Say we may be needing a signature later on and we want to be prepared so we don't lose any time. Then I want you both to go through all the statements and follow through on the board. Now that we know who we're looking for, see if there's a connection anywhere that we've missed. Try to find something, anything that would give an excuse to raid that house."

"Right, where will you be if we find something, boss?

"I'm going to buy a big bunch of flowers and congratulate the new mother and kiss the baby. I may even indulge in social chitchat with the midwife if she's still on duty. Ring me on my mobile if you find anything"

The office phone rang before he reached the door and was answered by Blake.

"MIT. Yes. Yes. I'll tell him." He replaced the phone.

"Boss, Elspeth Moran is downstairs. She has just confessed to the desk sergeant that she murdered her Husband."

Elspeth sat in the interview room with much the same demeanour as when they had first met her. She sat perched on the edge of the chair at a distance from the table with her hands clasped around her knees. She had replaced her thin wire spectacles and her hair was again tied back in a bun. She stared at the floor and did not look up at them when they entered the room. The constable who had been watching her stepped outside. Blake was immediately reminded of her description of the atmosphere her husband could create in their house. He could feel it now, a thick, black depression, so real it was almost physical.

Blake fitted the tapes into the machine and pressed the record button. Edwards began.

"This is a taped interview under caution with Mrs. Elspeth Moran On Monday 4th December at 5.35 p.m. Those present are Mrs. Elspeth Moran, Detective Inspector Edwards and Detective Sergeant Blake. Mrs. Moran, I must caution you that you are not obliged to say anything but that anything you do say may be used as evidence. Do you understand the caution?

For the benefit of the tape Mrs. Moran has nodded.

Mrs. Moran, would you prefer it if we postponed this interview until we can arrange legal representation for you?

For the benefit of the tape Mrs. Moran has shaken her head.

Mrs. Moran would you like a lady police officer to be present or a friend like Mrs. Parsons? I really do think you ought."

"No. It won't be necessary. I killed him. It's my fault." Her eyes never rose from the floor.

"So how did you kill him? Mrs. Moran?"

"I hit him on the head, in his office at school and he died."

"What did you hit him with?"

"A heavy blunt instrument, don't you read the papers, Inspector?" She looked up at him angrily. "I thought you were investigating my husband's death."

"I am, I am. Bear with me please. Can you describe this blunt instrument for me? What did it look like?"

"Don't you know? I thought you were in charge. It was big and heavy and I hit him with it." She lowered her eyes to the floor.

"I had to hit him, because he wanted me to have a child. I couldn't have a child so I hit him."

"When was this Mrs. Moran? When did you hit your husband?"

"Three years ago." She burst into tears, cradling her face in her hands.

"Mrs. Moran is not herself. Interview terminated at 5.45.pm.

"Just wait here a moment, will you Mrs. Moran? We won't be long."

Once on the corridor he directed the constable back into the room and turned to Bates.

"You checked her alibi, didn't you? Any doubt about it?"

"No, boss, she was two hours in the hairdresser's just like she said. They remember her. She's a regular. There's no way she could have done it."

"She's having a break down, not surprising really. Get the FME to her; he may have to put her in a place of safety. See if we can find out who her doctor is and get him out as well. Then get back to what I asked you to do."

29.

Katrina had had a difficult time and was in a side ward. The Irish staff nurse was being very protective and was standing no nonsense. He was a big baby and he had become distressed. The midwife had called in the duty doctor for a forceps delivery.

"She's exhausted and she's sleeping. I'm afraid I can't allow visitors tonight except for close relatives. You will have to come back tomorrow Inspector."

"Fine, I'll just leave these for her. Perhaps you'd see she gets them first thing, would you."

"Certainly!"

"The baby's alright is it? Only I was there when she started, she'd had a bit of a shock and Karen said she was a few days early."

"Mother and baby are both fine, just very tired. They need lots of rest. You know Karen Feeney then do you?"

"Well more her dad, Kevin, really. Is she still on duty? I wouldn't mind a having word with her if possible."

"Oh no, she doesn't work here any more she's on terminal leave. Well officially she doesn't finish until Friday, so she's still an employee, but she was owed annual leave and is taking it before she finishes. She got permission to do this one delivery because they are close friends."

"Right, well I still need a word, so I'll try and catch her at home then."

"If you're going there you might take her hat for her. It's very cold out and what with the baby and all she forgot it. I'll just get it from the staff cloakroom."

She return bearing a thick woollen bobble hat.

"And you're sure this is definitely hers are you? I wouldn't want to deprive somebody else of theirs." Gareth held his breathe.

"Oh, yes, she's been wearing that one to work for weeks. I'd know it any where."

"Oh, good," said Gareth, "Well I'll see that she gets it then."

Gareth drove outside the hospital gates and pulled over. He had switched off his mobile before he entered the hospital grounds to make sure it didn't interfere with any of their equipment. As soon a he switched back on it rang.

"Edwards."

"We've got the address," said Blake, "5. Alton Lane, off the Lichfield Rd. It's an upstairs Flat. The warrant is ready for signature once we have a reason for it. We've only found one thing that might be useful. Remember Paul Jarvis? He thought it was a bloke because he was wearing a woolly hat. We never found that hat. Do you want me to get OSG out again to search the lane and the bushes?

"No need little Sergeant," said Gareth with a chuckle, "I have it. She left it in the ladies at the Hospital. Put Highgate on standby and tell 'em it's urgent. I'm driving straight over there. I'll want any sort of match to connect it to that room; they can take their time with it after that. Have a SOCO team on standby as well. Tell them this takes precedence over routine. She's chucked in her job. After all that's happened she'll be thinking about leaving. Put Hardeep in a car outside her house now. If she leaves he's to follow her and call it in."

By 7 p.m. Edwards, a photographer and two Scene of Crime Officers were kicking their heels in the incident room at Mere Green. With them were two constables, one female, whom Edwards had requested from the duty inspector. Blake was sat in his car outside a magistrate's house in the Four Oaks district. 8 o'clock came and went increasing their restlessness and frustration. At 8.35 the phone rang. The lab at Highgate had found that three of the fibres recovered from Moran's room matched the hat. The hat had definitely, provably and demonstratively been in the room where Michael Moran had been killed. They also had plenty of ginger hairs that must belong to the owner of the hat. It was enough to justify the warrant. Edwards phoned Blake and ordered him to get the signature and meet them at Karen Feeney's flat. The Soco team had been briefed to secure finger prints, her toothbrush for DNA, any trainers, and any tracksuits on the premises. Edwards would arrest Karen Feeny and the two constables would then conduct her back to Mere Green to be held for questioning. Edwards, Blake and Singh would carry out a general search for documents, photographs, and any thing else which might assist in securing a conviction. The photographer would photograph everything.

"There's been no sign of movement since I got here," said Hardeep. "No lights on either."

There was no answer when they rang the bell. The uniformed constable opened the door with his enforcer and they all trooped upstairs and switched on the lights in every room. The place was in complete disarray. Drawers had been pulled out, cupboard and wardrobe doors had been left open. Karen Feeney had left in a hurry taking her suitcases and clothes with her.

The team carried on and did its work. They found a pair of flat soled shoes and the dark blue tracksuit, in a plastic rubbish bag in the loft, behind the cold water tank. The shoes were covered with orange muddy stains. There were pictures of Michael Moran and Karen. There were love letters from him in the desk drawer. They had everything they came for with the exception of Karen Feeney herself. However one bonus was her passport, also found in the desk drawer. Wherever Karen Feeney was going it wasn't out of the country.

Edwards knocked loudly on the door, which was opened by a sleepy Kevin in his pyjamas. "Kevin Feeney, I have reason to believe you may be harbouring Karen Feeney who is wanted for the murder of Michael Moran. I have a warrant to search these premises. Stand aside please."

When they were satisfied she wasn't there and hadn't been there. They made him dress and took him to Mere Green. Here they questioned him long into the night concerning her friends and relatives. They went through her address books with him looking for a possible location for her. Eventually in the early hours of the morning they drove him home. His world had collapsed completely. Edwards was very concerned for him. He was flat and sullen, completely depressed. He looked grey and drawn and ten years older. Edwards knew he couldn't leave him like this. Foremost in his mind was the thought that he might harm himself in this state. They had found references to an aunt in Solihull in Karen's address book. He left Hardeep with Kevin and went to meet Blake at the address. Blake had the warrant and the two uniformed constables with him. They had explained the situation and checked the place thoroughly. When they were sure Karen wasn't there and hadn't been there, they told Kevin's sister that he was in a bad way and asked if she'd go back and stay with him. She agreed and they drove her back to the school to relieve Hardeep.

Tuesday 5th December:

30.

Gareth arrived at the school at 9.55 a.m. He was bleary eyed having had just three hours sleep after the activity of the previous night. He had found the killer of Michael Moran and secured sufficient evidence to prove his case, but he had failed to capture the lady herself. Miss. Bailey had already arrived, and was waiting for him with Mr. Price in his office.

Edwards sat and took the invoice file out of his brief case. He wrote on the front of it for a minute in silence. Then he held it out to the finance officer.

"You will find all the goods obtained fraudulently from the school at those two addresses. Michael Moran was the thief. He was obsessed with fatherhood. He had attracted these two ladies and persuaded each of them to have a child with him. He set them up in residences which he also lived in on a part time basis and he furnished them. He was no better than a bigamist, except that he didn't actually marry them. The ladies concerned and their children are completely innocent. They had no idea of each others existence and each thought that they were Michael Moran's sole partner and that he had bought the goods lawfully. I am not sure whether you will be able to reclaim the property. You will have to raise this matter with fraud people, but somehow I don't think they will wish to proceed in a case where the only possible defendant who could be charged is already dead. I will put all this in writing for your superiors to make a judgement, but my advice to you is write it off. I doubt if the council would want the bad publicity it would get from making two single mothers and their children destitute. The best they could hope to do would be to regain a few sticks of furniture which they would end up auctioning off at probably less than half price."

Miss. Bailey took the file.

"Thank you Inspector. If it's as you say I think your assessment is probably correct. I doubt very much if the City Treasurer will want to proceed. We will have to look at our procedures and make sure this can't happen again, but that will probably be that. Those poor women! How awful for them!"

"It's not over yet, for them," said Gareth. "One of the properties was purchased with money defrauded from a building society. Joan Canfield will undoubtedly lose her home. They won't be so forgiving. They will almost certainly repossess. Both these women thought they had a future in a family with a man who loved them. They will now be single parents. Not an enviable position, Moran has done a lot of damage."

"Do you think he could have carried on like this, if he hadn't been killed? asked Price.

"Perhaps he might have continued for a while, but the man wasn't rational. He was consumed by his obsession and he was grooming other women for the same role. He could only have financed his activities by crime and he would have been caught eventually."

"Perhaps his killer did the female population a favour the?" said Miss Bailey. She was looking at him quite intensely. "Do you think you will catch him?"

"Her! It was a her. We know who she is. The whole world will know by the time the evening papers come out. Yes we will catch her in time. She is as much a victim as the others. He wronged her too, but she will spend many, many years in prison none the less. My job isn't always clear cut. The killer isn't always the guiltiest party. Did you ever meet Mr. Moran? In your finance capacity?"

"Yes, I quite liked him." Gareth noticed she was blushing.

"Well, you may have had a lucky escape there then." said Gareth grimly.

"We will be based at Mere Green for the next few weeks, Mr. Price, until this is all sorted out. So you can contact us there. We will be popping in from time to time to check details. I am giving you your finance office back today. We won't need it any more. I suppose you'll have a few problems until you can appoint a new bursar, so you'll need to get in there."

"I have my new bursar, Inspector." Mr. Price was beaming. "Miss. Bailey here has agreed to hand in her notice and to come and work for us in about a month's time. I can offer her a better salary than the Local Education Authority and from my point of view she is independent of the teaching staff and we can put the whole thing on a more professional footing."

Gareth stood to leave, but Price said, "Miss Bailey has to get back now, but I'd like another word with you Inspector. If you could wait a minute while I see her out? " Gareth nodded and sat down again.

When Price returned he was very sombre again.

"I've seen Kevin this morning. He's in bits. He told me about Karen. It's appalling, the damage Moran did. He's hurt everyone around him."

"Is his sister staying for a while?"

"He's gone back to Solihull with her. Thanks for fetching her; he's not fit for work. He's better over there. When the news breaks there'll be a lot of media pressure. I've ordered the staff to say nothing and refer the press to me. I'll make a brief statement and then refer them to you. I don't think he'll return. He's offered his resignation. I've told him to take time and think about it, but it's probably best all round if he does go. He'll probably go out to his daughter in Spain. They've been asking him to go for some time."

"What will you do for a caretaker?"

"The city is sending a mobile for the time being. We'll appoint again after a decent interval. There's something else I want to broach with you Inspector. It may sound a little callous, but life goes on, and in a school it has to go on very quickly. We can't sit on our hands here."

Gareth was bewildered and wondered what on earth was coming next. Price was different to the last time they had met. The anxious man had gone and the headmaster and his authority was back.

"You know this business with Gerard? I met him this morning and we've cancelled the debt. That bill will be paid with out further ado. I've wanted to get outdoor pursuits up and running here for sometime. He did a good job with that ski trip on the whole, despite the financial problem. He has a Mountain Leadership Certificate and I've asked him to get a sixth form trip up and running to Snowdonia at Easter. I don't want it to be just a school thing. I want some community involvement. Your wife told my wife that you are a hill walker?"

Edwards nodded his assent.

"I wondered if I could ask you to help out with the trip as voluntary instructor. Gerard will be in charge of course. There are other younger staff who would be interested; but he could do with experienced back up and I think you would be ideal."

Gareth was very taken aback but very flattered. The idea appealed to him immediately. When they had asked him to be a governor he had turned them down. He found the idea of attending policy meetings nauseating. This was different.

Monday 8th January

31.

The trail had gone cold. After a month of trying to trace Karen without success, it was time to move on. Gareth had decided to close down the incident room at Mere Green and pull back to Lloyd House. The case would remain open and subject to regular review but unless something new turned up there was nothing else they could do. Gareth was sitting with a fresh mug of coffee at the table in the incident room. He was leafing through one of two cold case files that had been sent over by Mills. Chief Inspector Mills was not one to let his officers sit on their hands for long. The first case was a 1980's throwback. Michael Shaunessy had been gunned down by an unknown gunman in the living room of his old people's bungalow in Falcon Lodge. They had never found the target. Every 12 months or so Mills dug the file out and gave it to one of his team to review. The notes of the various reviewing officers now amounted to nearly half of the file. It was probably a professional hit but there was no indication of why or who to date.

"End of the line for me then, Boss, is it?" asked Hardeep.

Bates and Singh were finalising their notes and written reports to pack away in the file boxes to be transported back to Lloyd house. Blake had also photographed the board as part of the record. The board had been pushed back and a constable was unplugging the television and video to take them back to wherever Hardeep had scrounged them from.

"I'm afraid so, Detective Constable Singh, back to burglaries, and muggings. Never mind, you need the experience. You have impressed though, and I've said so in my report. I may be calling for your services on secondment in the future, if that's alright with you."

"Too right, Boss, I'll come running. It's going to be a bit of an anti-climax going back to station work. It's a pity we didn't get her. It would have been nice to finalise things."

"We will boy, we will."

Looking down at the 20 year old files in his hands Gareth felt a twinge of unease and was suddenly not so sure. He had posted Karen as wanted and issued a warrant for her arrest. He had also issued a press release and had it circulated nationally with her photograph. There was no hiding place for Karen Feeny in the UK and he held her passport. She would need false papers to get out and she wasn't connected. A real criminal might have the contacts for that. Ordinary people don't. She could dye her hair, change her name start a new life but eventually she would make some slip and she would be back here sitting in front of him in an interview room. Nothing was more certain. He had to think like that. He had to be positive. They had been through her address book and visited all her friends, relatives and acquaintances, anyone who might have given her shelter. She had gone to ground somewhere and had evaded them. Someone must be helping her. There had to be someone they hadn't connected to her yet, but he was confident it wouldn't last. Not because that someone would give her up, but because of her, herself. He had looked into every detail of her life. She was just an ordinary everyday person, not a criminal, not a killer.

Circumstances had conspired against her and she would not be able to live with the result. When a normal person has done something heinous, no matter how justified, no matter what the consequences, the pressure on them to confess from their own inner selves is enormous. Good, ordinary honest people with a guilty secret reach a point were they cannot live with their guilt. It eats away at them bit by bit, day by day and in the end they want to be caught and sometimes engineer there own capture. The letter might come after a month or a year, or five years, but the letter usually came, or a telephone call, or 'there's a man at the front desk.' Only the criminally insane are unaffected by their own actions.

He opened the second of the two files. Vincent O'Hagan, found at the foot of the stairs of his house in Kingstanding. The body had been laid out to make it look like a fall, but the pathologist had said no. The neck had been broken manually by an expert. They were probably looking for a killer with military training.

"Post, Boss."

Blake handed him a plain white self-sealing envelope with a Spanish stamp. On the front was written 'F.O.A. Inspector Edwards', F.O.A. for the attention of. Now he was certain. He knew who it would be from. She had got out after all. He had received such letters in the past. He drank the last of the coffee and put the mug back on the table, and opened the envelope.

" *Dear Inspector Edwards,*

I could see that you recognised me that afternoon in the flat. You just didn't know that you had. I watched you with Katrina, so thoughtful, so careful, but hard and determined. You did what you had to do, but so gently. I knew then that you would find me. By now you will have connected me to my father and to Michael and you will know that I killed him. I didn't intend to, but I did and I want to tell you about it.

My relationship with Michael was the most wonderful thing that has ever happened to me. For few short months I was in heaven and thought that all my dreams of love and marriage and family would be fulfilled. We began before he divorced his wife, and he did promise me that he would divorce her. They had already been separated for years so I was not breaking anything up. I didn't tell my father, I knew he would be totally opposed to my having a relationship with a married man. When he found out he was furious and we did not speak again until recently. Gradually I came to realise that Michael had no real feelings for me. He wanted a child. He wanted me to have a child with him. I could have been anybody. He didn't care about me, just the idea of a child. I wanted commitment. I wanted him to divorce his wife and marry me. He just wanted me to get pregnant, so I stopped seeing him. It was so painful. I missed him so much. I had concentrated on him to the exclusion of others for nearly a year. When we finished I was totally alone. I didn't want to meet people. I just worked and stayed at home. Gradually I met and got together with some of my old friends again including Katrina. Katrina was so excited. She had met a new man and was very much in love. He was married but was divorcing his wife. He was going to marry Katrina and she was having his baby. We met at work a few times and then went out together. Eventually she invited me back to her new place. She had moved house since we were last friends. When I walked in, I was horrified. Everywhere I looked were pictures of Michael. How could I say anything? She would never believe me. She was convinced that he loved her and wanted me to meet him. I decided there and then that that would not happen. She was coming to the end of her time and I wanted me to deliver the baby. I couldn't refuse her but I was dreading meeting Michael.

I knew I had to confront him, not there with Katrina but by himself. I thought - 'perhaps he has changed. Perhaps he really does love her and its going to be alright.' - I didn't plan it. I just went to see him. The car park was full so I parked out on the road and walked round by my father's house across the playground and in through the far door. I didn't want to go through the front entrance and meet people and end up chatting. He was working in his office as I knew he would be at that time. I arrived just before four.

He was surprised to see me and smiled and it was like old times for a few minutes. Then I told him I was Katrina's friend and asked him what he was playing at. You see for the baby to be that far on, he must have started going out with her while he was still with me. He made her pregnant while he was still trying to get me pregnant. His attitude changed immediately. He threatened me and grabbed me by the left hand and squeezed it, digging his finger nails into my wrist. I asked him- 'do you love Katrina?' and he told me to mind my own business. I could tell then that he didn't. I said 'you're just using her, aren't you? You don't want her, just the baby.' He said if I said anything to Katrina he would tell her that I had tried to steal him from her; that I had tried to get him to dump her and the baby. His face was red and his eyes were bulging and then he laughed at me. He said I was jealous because I couldn't have his child. He said I was nothing; that I was rubbish. The callousness his words hit me like a fist. The skin on my face was cold. I felt small beads of sweat braking out on my forehead. My heart was racing. The increased blood pressure caused pain behind my eyes. I saw the statue of his dog on the table to my right and my hand found it. Almost without any decision I lifted it up above shoulder height. He sat at the desk half turned towards me, and looking up. Those laughing, taunting eyes became fearful as he realised what I was going to do. One hand started upwards to block me, but it was far too late. I brought it down on to his head. There was a dull and hollow thud like a hard ball hitting a wooden bat. The sparkle in his eyes dulled and he slumped forward. His head rested on the computer keyboard. I watched, fascinated as a small red trickle started and then suddenly it increased and spread across the keys on to the table and began to drip from the edge onto the floor.

My breathing was short and fast and there was pain in my chest, emotional not physical. It broke to my throat in a huge sob. My eyes stung with tears which blinded me. I stood there, unable to move, staring in horror at what I had not intended to do.

I came to myself again eventually. I had no idea how long I stood there, terrified, immobile, hearing only the ticking of the clock. It had never sounded as loud as it did now. It echoed in the silence of the room. A quarter past four, I knew I had to get away. The need to run was there at once, urgent, pushing me towards the door. I felt the blood pounding again and the beating in my head. I must get away; but I held back and forced thought and control upon myself. The corridor would be busy. The open holdall was there on the floor beside him. I pulled out his kit and thrust the statue into it and covered it with his towel. Then I changed into his track suit.

When I was ready I pulled the zip across. "Fingerprints" my brain said. I used my sleeve to wipe the door handle then opened the door just enough see through. There was no-one immediately outside. I waited, listening, listening. There was sound to my right, a gentle, rhythmic swishing moving away from me. The cleaner was sweeping down the corridor towards the outside door. To my left, there was the L-shape bend in the corridor. The mop in her bucket leaned against the wall next to her rubbish sack. I dropped the catch on the snap lock, still using my handkerchief. I listened again. The sweeping was still moving away down the corridor. I grabbed the bag and moved quickly through the door pulling it shut behind me, and sped for the corner. There were lots of people on the corridor and I just walked past them all bold as brass. If they could have heard my heart beating, to me it sounded like a drum. I went through the Tech. block and out the back and away.

I heard what you said to Katrina, about the other woman and I thought about his poor wife. I may not have intended to kill him, but I'm glad I did. I left my British Passport in the drawer for you to find, so that you would think you had me cornered. I thought that might give me some time. I was born here but my dad was born in Ireland so I have dual nationality. I travelled out on my Irish passport. I am here in Spain now with my elder sister.

It isn't that easy though is it? You probably know all about this. This thing is eating at me. I can't settle. I can't just forget about it. It is with me every minute of every day. I can't move on. I am stuck in a loop and it goes round and round. It's like a poem I did at school, "as idle as a painted ship upon a painted ocean." I'm in limbo. I need you to come and talk to me. We have to finish this. Will you come? Please come.

Karen Feeney.

8774302R0

Made in the USA
Charleston, SC
12 July 2011